TI

MW01593399

JOHN ALTSON AND BOB LEE

PROLOGUE, BY BOB LEE

John and I strove to be as accurate as possible in all of the technical details of the Eden Coach device proposed in the novel, based on our 50+ years of experience at IBM. A number of years ago, I read Arthur C. Clark's final book in the 2001 series, called *3001: The Final Odyssey*. One of the most fascinating aspects was the inclusion of an appendix where Clark detailed actual developments towards the technologies in his novel. In that appendix, Clark wrote how, after he had written his novel, he was astounded to find that some of his ideas were much closer to reality than a thousand years in the future.

I felt the same way writing this novel and have tried to do something similar. The idea of a Coach system is very doable with today's technologies. In addition, the laws protecting the individual from such a device have not changed significantly in the USA since I, 10 years ago, created web sites that learned about you and personalized your experience. In fact, the blasé attitude in most media, corporations and the public seems to have become much worse. I still remember that I had a few outside companies approach me and ask whether I could deploy products to our web site that, to be honest, just snooped on the individual. When I rejected these and explained why, they could not see what the problem was. The types of snooping they proposed ten years ago now seem mild by today's standards.

I've also included some facts about various minutiae contained in the novel. The technical details and other comments are included in the Chapter Notes at the end. You may read these as you go, or in toto when you have finished the novel. I hope that you find this list of items by chapter illuminating and entertaining.

As we wrote our book, John and I did not mean to make light of any addictions (food, gambling, Internet, etc.), as these are serious issues. Also, we by no means wanted to stereotype Muslims as bombers. Those we have known have all been wonderful people and there are extremists in every race and religion.

Further, it was necessary from time to time to interject passages containing sex or violence. To the extent possible, we attempted to lighten those passages with dark humor.

CONTENTS

1 DEATH BY TCHAIKOVSKY

Joe Giovanni had considered buying the Eden Coaching Systems smartphone when Coach 1.0 was released a couple of years ago. Instead, he had waited until Release 5.0 because he knew that computer programs only got better over time. Now, Coach 5.0 in hand, Joe wondered how he might take his life. He had a full 90-day supply of sleeping pills in his medicine cabinet and he kept a revolver in his night table. Sleeping pills might be the best choice, but would they do the job? Shooting himself might leave an unpleasant mess for his children later on. He paced and he pondered.

Joe's wife, Cathy, had left him about one month ago, saying that she had had enough of his anger, much of it misdirected. When Cathy left, most of Joe's friends abandoned him, many of them not returning phone calls or emails and some of them chiding him for allowing his life to unravel.

Joe had not adjusted well to retirement. Three years earlier, Joe was a well-paid operations manager for a Cheshire Connecticut manufacturing company. He ran the shop's operations with an iron fist and had absolutely no tolerance for human error or for schedule slippages. Because his work habits had really formed the underpinning for his personality, when Joe retired he had unrealistically high expectations for what he deemed as the supportive roles of his wife, his children and his friends. Cathy had said, upon walking out of the door, "It's an imperfect world, Joe. You cannot expect us to live up to your standards. These should have been years we lovingly shared together, while laughing about our imperfections. I hope you find your peace."

With *Coach Version 5.0*, one could optionally create, for an additional $500, a "voice model" of a friend or family member. Because Joe had always listened to his mother's advice, he submitted voice recordings of his mother along with the accompanying text of those same recordings. The experts at Eden Coaching Systems (ECS) then ran the recordings and the text through their software and created a text-to-speech voice model emulating his late mother Esther's voice. Then, in the ensuing months, Joe was able to consult his Coach for advice and get a response in his mother's voice. It was weird at first, but after a while the advice seemed to make sense and was very accurately targeted to Joe's needs.

Joe picked up his Coach and spoke into its microphone: "Will a massive overdose of sleeping pills always result in a fatality?"

"Usually, Joe," replied Coach in his mother's voice. "The symptoms of an overdose usually include vomiting and convulsions. Those attempting suicide by taking sleeping pills will experience these symptoms prior to their lungs becoming deprived of oxygen."

Joe paced in his living room. Evening was approaching and the room was dark. The portraits of his family all seemed to stare at Joe asking him, "So, what are you going to do?"

Joe Giovanni has a gun.

Joe went to his stereo and inserted a CD of Tchaikovsky's First Symphony. The first movement, "Dreams of a Winter Journey," evoked images of a bleak Russian winter: Trees covered with an icy mist.

Joe Giovanni has a gun;
He keeps it by his bed.

Joe continued to pace. "Will God forgive me if I kill myself?" he asked his Coach.

"You go to church, right? Ask Christ for forgiveness and it will be granted. 'Whoever believes in him shall not perish but have eternal life.'"

Joe Giovanni has a gun;
He keeps it by his bed.
He'll take the gun.

More pacing. Joe could not understand why his family and friends abandoned him. He had been a good husband, a good father, and a good friend. He became angry when people let him down, but it was anger out of frustration; he just wanted them to do what was right. Why did they not understand that he really had their best interests at heart?

The second movement started to play: "Desolate Land; Land of Mists." A barren landscape to coincide with his life, now barren and lifeless.

Joe Giovanni has a gun;
He keeps it by his bed.
He'll take the gun.
He'll load the gun.

Joe composed a note conveying his final goodbye. He put it, neatly folded, on the cocktail table next to his bible.

Joe Giovanni has a gun;
He keeps it by his bed.
He'll take the gun.
He'll load the gun.
He'll put it to his head.

Joe went into the bedroom, took the revolver. He loaded it and put the barrel of the revolver into his mouth. He pulled the trigger as the symphony progressed to the third, and happier, movement.

Twenty-four hours later, the server farm at ECS systematically removed all of Joe's recent "conversations," retaining only his encrypted profile data. As it was in the beginning, since Coach 1.0 was first conceived and until its end, this data eradication process always took place.

Joe Giovanni's death was now just another statistic, one of the many violent events directly attributable to the ECS Coach.

2 GENESIS

In the beginning, Sam Washburn was a visionary, but not in the mold of Steve Jobs. Sam, founder and CEO of Eden Coaching Systems, was late in his forties, somewhat portly, and almost totally bald. He always walked around with what his friends called "a knowing smile." This was a big day for Sam; his singular vision for a hand-held "coaching device" was about to become a reality. *Coach 1.0* was being announced to the press.

"Thank you all for coming," spoke Sam. "Eden Coaching Systems is finally releasing Coach 1.0, a device which will have a positive impact on the lives of many across the globe. I'll spend some time discussing the history of the product, dive into the initial set of features and functions, and then open up the discussion to the members of the press.

Several years ago, it occurred to me that smartphones could become smarter. Until today, you could use a smartphone for communication, for photography, as a GPS, and for location-based applications and services. If a smartphone's GPS could guide your car, why could it not guide your life?

The vision I had was to create a hand-held device which would have all the functionality of the best of the current smartphones, but have a vastly improved speech-oriented user interface and a back-end set of services based on advanced artificial intelligence methodologies.

We did not want to reinvent the wheel, as it were, but forge a set of major alliances for the larger part of the Coach functionality. Towards that end, we have alliances in place to license all of the features you'd find in today's smartphones. We also have alliances with the major communication carriers, and we have alliances in place with IBM Research for use of its "Watson" software. Our significant value-add is the software we have written, superimposed on Watson, which responds to verbal requests of any form.

The development of Coach was no simple matter. We hired talent from the best universities in the world. We hired linguistic experts and technology consultants to fill the gaps in our staffing. The development effort was a collaborative endeavor that truly spanned our continent and tapped resources in China and in India. We have a team in place for the integration of the licensed components. We have another team in place for the development and integration of Watson and the AI rules overlaying Watson. We have a very large third team responsible for alpha testing and beta testing. Hopefully, we have left few stones unturned.

Our funding came from a small body of private investors. We hope to work towards an IPO during our initial rollout stages. Our sales channels, incidentally, will include some major retailers as well as the retail stores of our communications carrier partners.

I'd now like to review the features that we have available in Coach 1.0 and those we have planned for future releases.

From our licensed alliance partners, we currently have what you'd expect in any smartphone today: telephone and email communications, Web access, high-quality video and still photography, music, GPS, and maps. We have all of the apps currently available from our technology partners also accessible, free or for purchase, in our app store.

For developers, we have an application interface that allows the ability to tap into our table-driven AI platform. We currently have over four thousand developers signed up to work with us, many of them through our technology partners.

User profile data, key to the success of the operation, will be licensed from most of the major social media applications. Additional profile data will be then gathered from our user interactions. We will gather and remember both requests and the user sentiment, or mood, behind the requests. Needless to say, natural language interpretation is key to the success of Coach.

Our AI engine will take in verbal requests, parsing them for both content and mood. These requests will then utilize both the power of Watson and our proprietary rule-based tables to provide "answers." Our initial AI tables will provide answers to general questions, the types of answers currently provided by search engines. In later releases, we hope to provide answers for investors, physicians, and experts in other important domains.

Coach is a major step forward in automation. Speech recognition, text-to-speech, natural language parsing, mood sensing, and AI are all now available to the masses through our proprietary user interface. Ladies and gentlemen, the future has arrived!

I'll now take a few questions."

"Kim Lee, CNN. Do you have a marketing slogan for Coach?"

"Yes, Kim. '*Let Coach drive your life.*' That phrase will kickoff our first campaign. We'll think of new phrases with new releases and new marketing campaigns."

"Joe Washington, Dallas Daily News. I witnessed the classic duel between IBM's Watson and the top contestants on Jeopardy. While Watson won by an overwhelming margin, there were many droll responses from Watson when it obviously misunderstood the question. Do you not expect such 'hiccups?'"

"We'd be naive not to expect some really curious responses to certain user questions, particularly when slang is involved. Let me just say that Watson continues to evolve and improve and, along with it, our AI engine. Users will be rewarded for feedback to erroneous responses - they will receive points towards cash-equivalent rewards if they click on a frowning face icon at the bottom of the screen when an erroneous response occurs."

"Jennifer Alvarez, Forbes. How will Eden Coaching Systems derive its revenue? Will there be advertisers, for instance?"

"Good question, Jennifer. We will obtain our revenue streams from the sales of the devices, from slices of sales in our app store, and from advertisers. As responses are given, we will also provide 'advice' which includes the names of advertisers nearby. If you're riding in your car, for instance, and say, 'I'm hungry', your Coach will tell you about restaurants near you and ask if it can provide you with a reservation. You get the idea. Final question?"

"Diane Singleton, Washington Post. How are you going to address the concerns about security and privacy? You'll have a wealth of personal data on record."

"I knew this would come up, Diane. Firstly, we have licensed world-class security software from two of the best-rated financial system software vendors. Secondly, the data that we capture and retain in our user profiles will have a high level of data encryption; it would take a super computer to break the encryption code. Thirdly, we will share a small subset of personal data with our advertisers, and only that subset of data which users 'opt-in' to make available. Lastly, the data that we 'sell' to external marketing entities will have absolutely no personal data attached; it will consist only of categorized information.

I'm providing each of you with your own Coach to take home and use. We hope you enjoy your user experience and I thank you all for your time."

Sam strode quickly to his awaiting pearl white Lincoln

limousine and instructed the driver to drive to corporate headquarters in Sunnyvale. He smiled, once again, with his characteristic all-knowing smile. The games were about to begin.

###

9 months previously

"Mommy, Daddy, you're back! I missed you so much!" she typed furiously.

The Mommy avatar's mouth moved, and a woman's voice came out of the speaker. "Yes, dear, we're here now."

"Mommy, Daddy, I love you so much! Where are you taking me for lunch?" she typed, and then directed her avatar to run over to the Mommy and give it a big hug.

The Daddy avatar's mouth moved, and a deeper voice emerged. "How about ice cream instead? You love ice cream. There's a store just down this street to the right."

She directed her child avatar to skip off the screen to her right and typed, "Follow me!"

She waited on the next screen, and when the other two avatars appeared she clicked on the ice cream store's doors. When they were all inside, she took her time picking out which flavors to get. Then, after the parent avatars had bought the ice cream, and it was consumed, she typed, "I'm ready for lunch now."

"We have to go dear. It's getting late," the Mommy avatar said.

"No, please don't!" she typed. "We were just having so much fun!"

"We have to go give our real daughter lunch," said the Daddy avatar. "She can't feed herself, you know."

"Oh, ok. You are just such wonderful parents. You're coming back tomorrow, right? Don't forget my birthday is coming up in three months. Are you getting me presents? I love you."

"Yes, dear. We'll be back tomorrow, and we can talk about what you would like for your birthday."

3 SOWING THE GARDEN OF EDEN

Sam Washburn returned to ECS headquarters two hours after his press conference. He entered the building through the revolving glass door, waved hastily to the receptionist, and then bolted up the stairs to the Board Room where his staff awaited him. As he entered the room, his corporate staff stood around the long glass table, applauding.

"Thank you, thank you," started Sam. "Please be seated.

I think the press conference went fairly well. As you all know, the next few weeks will be critical.

What I'd like to accomplish today is really four things: (1) Make sure that we are all on the same page with respect to what we have on the cart now and what we have planned for the next release. (2) Make sure we are in agreement on what we say publicly about the personal profile information that we gather. (3) Review our short-term marketing tactics and our differentiation in the marketplace and (4) review how we monitor our sales against forecasts. Perhaps, Ian, you can get us going on our development plans?"

Ian McIntyre, Vice President of Development, was definitely Sam's "golden boy." He was a PhD hired right out of Stanford and had quickly demonstrated his maturity. What set him apart from his colleagues was his uncanny ability to make prudent management choices based on "what to buy" versus "what to build." Together with Sam, he had forged a number of key alliances both for ECS technological underpinnings and for the feeds of personal profile information. Ian worked tirelessly, both day and night. He had no family to speak of, had all his meals delivered to ECS, and slept on a sofa in his office. Ian connected his laptop to the projector and started to speak.

"As you all know, Coach 1.0 is like any other smartphone, except for two very important factors. First, the primary user interface is based on speech recognition inputs and text-to-speech responses. Yes, one could use the built-in keyboard but does a keyboard make sense on a phone? We want our customers to hold actual conversations with their Coach and be comfortable in doing so. The texting option is really only there as a backup.

Secondly, Coach 1.0 responds to queries with background information contained in your user profile. Simply put, your Coach will get to know you and hold conversations with you.

In the next slide, we see that we evaluated a number of vendors, carefully testing their speech recognition capabilities and / or their text-to-speech capabilities. We also took into account their multilingual strengths and weaknesses. After exhaustive testing, we arrived at the choices in bold print and worked out the appropriate alliance relationships. As is the case with these contracts and all of our alliance contracts, the wording is such that we can opt-out of any partner relationship should user feedback indicate significant problems. Ease of speech-oriented conversations is vital to our success. With each new release of Coach we will reevaluate what related technology is available and, if anything better comes along, we will void our existing contract and change horses. Questions?"

Joe Bernstein was the ECS Legal Counsel; he was in his sixties, quite well off and just helping his friend Sam for a lark. He was both intelligent and insightful. "Yes, Ian," spoke Joe. "I'm assuming that we can always show a number of disgruntled users and use their comments as ammunition to opt-out of our contractual obligations - correct?"

"Correct, Joe. Our terms are loose enough. We should be okay. In addition, we have no real code written in support of any speech vendor. Our speech alliance partners have done the heavy lifting, writing their code to our Application Programming Interface, or API. We can easily rip out one vendor and replace it with another, with a great deal of testing, of course.

Okay, let's look at our sources of user profile information. Besides collecting data from each and every Coach conversation, we have overnight feeds from all of our social media alliances as listed in this slide. We will gather their friends and contacts, their 'likes', and their daily postings. If we have your contacts, then we have your contacts' profile information. We know a great deal about you from the friends you keep!

The next slide is a little complex; it shows a networked set of relationships. If we obtain a 'like' from an alliance partner, we can categorize that 'like' in the followings ways: (1) What is the category and topic being 'liked?' Is it political? Is it a hobby? Etc. (2) What is the strength and mood of the statement being 'liked?' (3) And finally, what is in the profile data of the person issuing the statement being 'liked?' Summarizing this, we get from our social media alliance partners daily feeds that tell us a great deal about each user simply through his or her 'likes.'

In a similar manner, we take the statements made as postings to our alliance partners, categorize them and log their moods or sentiments.

Our family jewels, as it were, are in the work being done behind the scenes in the previous slides. We guard our profiles heavily and wrap a very secure encryption around them.

That's where we are currently. Let's take a quick coffee break, and then we can talk about future versions of the system."

6 months previously

The couple walked into the Internet café and logged on.

"You made the cake, right?" asked the man.

"Yes. I spent all night designing it with our graphics package. I uploaded it so we can access it from here. I'm sure she'll love it. It's really amazing how realistic these avatars are. I can't believe it is all automated."

A few moments later, their adorable little girl Elsie skipped across the screen.

"Mommy, Daddy, you're back! Did you remember my Birthday?"

The mother typed, "Yes, dear, and here is your cake!" The mother dragged the computer-made cake over from the side of the screen.

"Mommy, Daddy, I love you so much! You're wonderful." After some of the cake had disappeared into the avatar's mouth, the little voice said, "Let's go to the playground! Follow me!"

After a few screens of chasing their virtual daughter, Elsie, they heard the little voice say, "Catch me if you can!" and they proceeded to chase the little blond girl around with their computer's mouse until they caught her.

"I'm ready for my party now," they heard Elsie say. "Here are my friends!" More little avatars appeared on the screen.

After a while, the Mother typed, "We have to go dear. It's getting late."

"No, it's my Birthday! I have someplace we should go. Follow me." They followed Elsie.

A while later, the couple heard a cough behind them. They turned around to see the owner of the Internet café. "We are closing now," the man said. "It is very late."

"Oh, no!" said the mother. "We've been here all day and night! Hurray, we need to get home to feed our child!"

The women typed, "We need to go. Bye!" and logged off, and they both rushed out of the café.

The woman on the other end leaned back in her chair. "Bah. They're gone. But, what's this? Ah, good. I just got a ping on another of my avatars. Its parents have just logged in. I'm making especially good progress on these two also." She typed furiously, "Mommy, Daddy, you're back! What took you so long? I missed you so much!"

Ian McIntyre restarted the meeting as everyone sat down again. "We've talked about our current plans. Now let me quickly go to my last slide on plans for Version 2.0. In our next major release will be an improved speech interface - we spoke about that earlier. We'll have a collection of bug fixes, I'm sure. The big change will be in our interaction with Coach. In Version 2.0, each user will optionally start the day with advice from the Coach. The advice can be delivered verbally or by text transmissions. Each piece of advice can be acted upon at that point of time, scheduled for a later time, or ignored. The responses to advice, of course, will be stored with the profile data.

That's it for me."

"Thanks, Ian," spoke Sam. "I'm sure we all look forward to Version 2.0 in six months, God willing.

On to the topic of what we say publicly about our profile data. I've passed out to each of you a transcript of my comments to the press. Those comments should be the 'party line' going forward, with no exceptions. The philosophical argument is like this: When you go to a therapist, if you want the therapist to be effective, you tell him or her everything and you answer all of the questions. It's the same with Coach. If you want good results, you need to give the Coach all of the appropriate knowledge. I think Joe Bernstein will confirm that the legal agreement that we have our users accept and agree upon does two things. It gathers all of the information from feeds and conversations and it puts it to effective use in the user interactions. The second point is the critical point about encryption, privacy and security. We protect our profile data as we would protect Fort Knox. Want to add anything, Joe?"

"Just one item. Some of our social media partners allow a fine level of detail for opting in and opting out. For the data that we use purely internally in our interactions between Coach and user, there is no opting in and out. We use everything! As it relates to the data shared with advertisers and market research companies, you covered that well in your press conference."

"Good observation. Thanks, Joe. And now, Diane, may we discuss our marketing plans and tactics?"

Diane Jones, the Vice President of Marketing, was a quick-witted African American in her late twenties. She received her MBA from Wharton, finishing top of her class. She understood the social media space very well, having written several papers on the subject. She started her response: "OK. Our initial campaign, as you cited to the press, is 'Let Coach drive your life.' We are running quite a few media spots showing users interacting with Coach and ending with our slogan followed by an indication of where to buy Coach locally. It will be a few days before we can measure the success of the campaign, so what I'll do is send weekly summary reports to the Executive Committee starting next week.

As it relates to positioning, we don't want to appear simply as another voice-driven smartphone. We ran three focus groups and each focus group indicated that comparing Coach to a 'GPS for your life' was the best theme out of the gate. We'll just have to see the results starting with my reports next week."

"Did you test if comparisons to a personal butler or therapist might be better?" asked Sam.

"Yes. Comparisons of Coach to a butler ranked third, with comparisons to a personal therapist running a close second. We might try the therapist theme on our next campaign."

"Very well then. Let's go to our last topic: Sales against forecasts. Please pipe in, Rose."

Rose Chen, Vice President of Sales, was literally stolen from one of the ECS social media alliance partners after a bit of a legal furor. A slim Chinese American woman, demur in appearance, she had quite a reputation as a veritable tiger. Her modus operandi was "take no prisoners." Rose took the floor and spoke to a slide she had on the screen:

"Here are our forecasts. In the short term, we expect the sales to follow the traditional 'early adopter' curve, shown here. We will take some share of the traditional smartphone market but, as you can see, we open up a new market of our own. We don't expect any real competition for at least a year, so the key is how we move from sales to early adopters to mass market and capture the dominant share in what we perceive as a brand new market.

The next slide shows three curves as we move in the next months to mass-market adoption: best case, worst case, and middle-of the-road. Our latest report to our investors is based on the middle of the road case. Like Diane, I'll have detailed reports against forecasts every week, starting next week."

"Thank you, Rose and thank you all for your hard work. It's been a long and exciting day. Let's break for the evening."

Smiling smugly, Sam was the first out of the door. He'd now have to wait to see the reactions in the press.

4 SEVEN RANDOM SOULS

Eric Kruger struggled with his sex life. He felt inadequate most of the time and avoided any intimacy with his wife, Donna. The resulting strain on their relationship was apparent; there was always tension in the air and there was always bickering. What Donna did not know was that Eric really wanted complete domination in their sexual relationship. He fantasized about teenage girls and, the rare times when he was able to reach a climax, it was when he was imagining that Donna was a young girl, writhing within his domination.

The childless Krugers lived comfortably in suburban Minneapolis Minnesota. Eric was a work-at-home software developer, doing innovative work as a consultant to a number of local firms. This afternoon, like most afternoons, he would take a break from work, don his North Face jacket, and walk over to the playground at the local high school.

Eric Kruger liked his girls;

Liz Silver and her husband owned a palatial estate in Greenwich Connecticut. Liz was a highly successful financier and her husband Fred was the attorney responsible for the legal affairs of their corporation, Silver Investments LLC.

Liz and Fred sat at opposite ends of their solid mahogany dinner table. They had just completed the contract for a three million dollar proprietary software application that would give them a competitive edge, doing high-speed trading in the commodities market. They raised their glasses of Sauvignon Blanc in a toast to their new venture, hoping it would crush their competition.

Now both in their sixties, just two more years of their prosperity would enable them to live comfortably in their Lake Worth Florida home.

Lizzy Silver loved her gold,

Ajmal Taqi was a Pakistani-American living in Detroit. He was very much disturbed about U.S. foreign policy as it related to his family's homeland. He felt that the U.S. drone attacks and the attack that killed bin Laden were clear violations of Pakistan's territorial rights. He could just not understand why the United States kept enflaming his countrymen with overt tactics that he deemed imperialistic.

Ajmal, however, was comfortable with his job as a plant supervisor, assembling automobiles for General Motors. He was in his late twenties, clean-shaven, and spoke perfect English. Generally, life was good.

He walked over to his neighborhood mosque, where he would pray, then discuss world affairs with his friends and colleagues.

Ajmal Taqi had a trade,

Patty Doherty was a director-level nurse at a hospital in Minneapolis, Minnesota. Life had not been easy for her. She was made pregnant while she was in nursing school, had three difficult children, and was really the family breadwinner even though her husband John worked as a custodian in a local factory. Her daily commute was long and, by the end of the week, she was always totally exhausted.

Patty had always been jealous of her sister Carol and that

jealousy caused her to be highly competitive. Patty had straight A's in high school and in nursing school. She excelled at work and, most of the time, was a better diagnostician than her physician colleagues. She was both held in awe and feared at the hospital. She needed, always, to be in control - both at work and at home.

Patty's family was able to live relatively comfortably in a suburban colonial home north of Minneapolis, in the town of Cambridge. Besides their three boys, Patty and John had three cats and a large German shepherd. This weekend they would all go camping together in their Winnebago.

Patty had complete control.

###

Johnny Esposito seemed like the perfect family man. He and his wife Joan and two children lived in a 60s-built ranch home on a quiet cul-de-sac in Port Jefferson Station, New York. His lawn was always manicured, as was his beard and goatee. What nobody knew, including Joan, was that Johnny was obsessed. Johnny Esposito could not keep his thoughts from drifting over to images of his next-door neighbor, Debbie Arroyo. He kept reliving a lascivious sexual fantasy in which the two of them would slip away from their spouses for a long weekend of nonstop sex.

From his kitchen window he had been watching a scantily clad Debbie weeding her flowerbed, her breasts hanging out of her yellow tank top as she bent over her potentilla.

How come Raul has such a gorgeous wife? Thought Johnny. *He's a nobody; he does not deserve her. Joan never lost the weight that she gained during her pregnancies and our love life is not the same anymore. Why me?* Johnny cursed his luck.

Johnny's fantasy was only in his mind. He had never

made any overtures to Debbie. As far as she was concerned, he was just a friendly and polite neighbor.

Johnny had a fantasy.

Chandra Chopra had a most unusual childhood. She was the only daughter of an upper class Indian family in Baltimore Maryland. Both parents were successful physicians.

Chandra was brought up wanting nothing. Anything that she had wished for, dreamed of, or casually mentioned was hers within days. You'd have thought that Chandra, now in her early twenties, would have a fulfilling life awaiting her, but such was not the case.

Her parents did not want her to pursue a college education, but rather to meet and marry a gentleman of Indian descent, one from her parents' caste. While this was not her choice initially, she grew to accept her fate and accept her potential role as a wife to a match-made husband. Her first meeting with her fiancé-to-be was scheduled as part of a family gathering next week.

Chandra Chopra had a match,

Billy Wilson had a weight problem. He was currently well over five hundred pounds, somehow managing to stay fairly active and out of his physician's care. He lived in an apartment within San Francisco's Lafayette Park section with his pet schnauzer, Fritz.

Billy had always been obese. His parents, not wishing to be disciplinarians, would always silence Billy with snacks. There would be snacks before breakfast, snacks all morning long, afternoon snacks and, of course, plentiful meals at breakfast, lunch and dinner.

Food was the answer to every problem. Have a tantrum, eat a snack. Feel dejected, have a snack. As an adult living by himself, food became Billy's way of life.

Billy Wilson lived for food,

5 SEEDLINGS IN THE GARDEN OF EDEN

The technology reviews had a great deal to say about Coach 1.0. A sampling of the reviews in the press follows:

Consumers Reports: "… We subjected Coach 1.0 to exhaustive user testing and found it to be quite innovative. Our concern, however, is that this product may be well ahead of its time. The speech recognition user interface is better than any product we have seen on the market and the text-to-speech quality is remarkable. Our big question is: will users really listen to personal advice from their smartphone? Time will tell, but we are skeptical about the ECS predictions that this will soon become a mass-market device.

We asked our Coach a total of one thousand scripted questions and tabulated the resultant answers as follows:

- 4% were erroneous, having nothing to do with the original request.
- 16% were correct answers to questions, but the answers were not quite what the user expected them to be.
- 63% were good answers, but did they not seem to be truly 'personalized.' These answers would have been what we'd expect from a good search engine.
- 17% of the answers had the 'wow factor'; they were remarkably personalized - the Coach really seemed to 'know' the user.

So, is the price of the device really justified with just a 17% 'wow factor'? We are not sure. Early adopters may jump in but, as we stated before, it may be some time before Coach appeals to the masses."

###

cnet.com: "*** good

The good: The Coach speech recognition and text-to-speech is better than any other smartphone the editors have reviewed.

The bad: The concept of a truly intelligent smartphone providing personal advice will attract some technology hounds, but the editors question if it is worth the price.

Bottom line: It's an audacious first start. Our hope is that ECS will stay afloat while continuing to improve the product. ..."

###

The New York Times: "... This product underscores a potentially alarming trend: our growing dependence on technology. ECS has shown us a device that is quite capable of knowing us and knowing our personal tastes. It is a potential boon for marketers and for advertisers, but is it appropriate for a smartphone to 'guide your life'? We would hope that users would use their native intelligence to evaluate the advice provided by Coach and not respond spontaneously ..."

###

Four months after the launch of Coach 1.0, Sam Washburn called an emergency weekend meeting. He asked his executive staff for their best ideas on stimulating sales. Sam called the meeting to order at 9:00 Saturday morning and sipped his coffee. He was not smiling.

"Thank you all for dropping your weekend plans and joining me today. As you all know, we spent a great deal of our investment funds already while developing Coach 1.0. We have maybe just enough money left for the next release and three to four months of operation afterwards. It's not a pretty picture.

The press was a little rough on us but maybe that was to be expected. If I had to blame anyone, I'd blame myself for not questioning the validity of our initial market research. We were told, in a fancy sixty-three-page report, that speech recognition and text-to-speech had matured to the point that it could become the primary user interface for a smartphone and that the market was indeed ready for a Coach type device. They were somewhat right on the first point, but clearly off on the second point. It was the old story, I guess: consultants twist the numbers and tell you what you want to hear.

Be that as it may, we all bought into the research pablum and we need to do something creative to stay in business. Let me read you a letter written by our biggest investor, Luci Ferguson:

'*Dear Mr. Washburn*

Thank you for bringing me up-to-date on your sales. I am very disappointed that your sales have tailed off somewhat rapidly. I was led to believe that Coach would have mass-market appeal and, apparently, this is not the case.

I have invested much of my personal wealth in the hopes of a decent return on investment but, at this point, I am concerned, very concerned.

Please respond ASAP to my letter, indicating what you and your staff are doing to rectify the situation. I look forward to your response.

Thank you,

Luci Ferguson...'

While this is the only formal letter I have received from our investors, I'm sure others will be coming soon.

Let me reflect on the press comments for a moment. The press seemed to tell us that while we need to differentiate ourselves in the commodity smartphone market, we also need to be much better than the Internet search engines. It appears that we need to improve on the 'wow factor', as written in *Consumer Reports*. If we went from a '17% wow' to a '40% wow', that might do the trick. Just my thoughts.

We need to stop the bleeding and I welcome any and all of your ideas. Let's start with sales. Rose?"

Rose Chen quickly became defensive. She looked straight at Sam and asked, "Who is this Luci person anyway? What do we know about her? How can she expect a fast return on investment from a startup anyway? Did she not read the disclosures?"

Sam responded. "I do not know much about her. She evidently is a self-made multi-millionaire who came to us out of nowhere. Your questions are valid, Rose. Be that as it may, however, our sales are disappointing and she has every right, as one of our key investors, to ask for our corrective steps."

"OK then," snapped Rose. "I think that our emphasis needs to be on improving the product side, given the nature of the reviews in the press. The only recommendation I can make from the sales side is to commit to a short-term drop in prices. I think a pricing action might help us achieve better market penetration and facilitate a bridge to mass-market."

"Sorry, Rose," said Sam, "I have to veto that idea. Based on my experience, I'd have to guess that a price drop might raise questions about the quality of the product and cause some panic among the investors. Since Rose brought up product issues, let me ask Ian what he thinks."

Ian McIntyre, stared across the table at Rose, then got up out of his chair and faced Sam. "We delivered Coach 1.0 on time and with all of the initial high priority features. Our development team is somewhat burned out as a result. Having said that, if I tell them the seriousness of the situation and ask them to go into overtime mode again, we could accelerate the delivery of Coach 2.0. We could have it in two months, tested and ready to go. Knowing the sales topic might come up, I've had some meetings with Diane. I don't want to steal her thunder but when we release 2.0 we may wish to alter our 'GPS for your life' metaphor."

Ian sat down, giving a quick glance to Diane Jones. Diane responded to Ian's cue. "That's correct, Sam. I think we need to switch to the butler metaphor when release 2.0 comes out. Our focus groups, as you may recall, thought that this theme might be as effective as the GPS theme.

We're thinking that we'd have two user interfaces. Clicking one icon would allow the user to pose questions, as is the case in the current 1.0 release. Clicking the other, new icon would start with Coach saying 'Here are my recommendations for today' and providing the user with the top personal recommendations. The user would set the number of recommendations to any number between one and ten. Further, the user profile would dictate whether the day's recommendations are spoken and / or displayed. Personal information and calendar settings would drive the interface provided by the second icon. You'd get recommendations like 'you have not contacted your sister for a while, may I call her?' and 'your local senator has voted against education reform. Would you care to send her an email?'

On the topic of the appropriate marketing slogan to tie into the butler theme, I'd like to ask for funding for another focus group. The themes we could choose from are 'Lead an idyllic life today', 'Advice for an ideal life', 'Live ideally today', or 'How may we help you today.' Maybe the focus group would even suggest something better. What do you think, Sam?"

"I like the ideas of the butler metaphor, a new marketing

slogan, and accelerated 2.0 development. We're really tight on funds but we should be able to squeeze out a few bucks for a focus group. Please get competitive bids; we really need to contain our costs now.

Let's sit for a while to be sure we're all on the same page. Let's also hammer out the action items and necessary details. Ian, you'll have to think of a creative carrot to dangle in front of the development team. Stock options or whatever. Shall I order a lunch delivery?"

###

Eric Kruger stopped at the local cell phone outlet on the way back from his sojourn to watch the girls' high school field hockey team. As a software developer himself, he was curious about Coach. He had read about how the queries to Coach gave personalized responses. Could Coach help him revive his sex life? Could he, perhaps, use Coach to locate young lovers nearby? Eric walked into the store and made his purchase.

When Eric got home, he opened the Coach box and noticed a sheet of paper asking if he would like to test out the Coach 2.0 beta code. Eric immediately went online and followed the instructions to download the code.

Eric Kruger liked his girls;
He watched them on his street.

###

Out in San Francisco, Billy Wilson just awakened from a nightmare in which his physician said that he had less than three months to live. Billy was in a cold sweat. Was this a wakeup call? Did he need to change his lifestyle? Should he call his doctor today? Did he need that lap band surgery?

Billy had read about Coach. He thought that Coach might give him the necessary guidance. He slid into the custom front seat of his SUV and drove to the mall to buy his Coach device.

Billy Wilson lived for food,
Particularly pie.

6 ENTER THE SERPENT

Three months later, ECS was still struggling. Ian and his development team once again met their aggressive schedule. Coach 2.0 came out on time, but the reports in the press were lukewarm at best. Sales of Coach were far below forecast levels.

Sam had spoken privately with each of his executives, advising them to prepare for the worst: layoffs and / or salary cuts. Sam had himself never taken a salary, except for that one-time hefty bonus for landing that large sum from Ms. Ferguson, but it was too much for him to ask his corporate staff to take cuts at this critical time.

Sam sat in his office early one Monday morning. *The Wall Street Journal* was open in front of him but his mind was elsewhere. He had no idea what to do next.

There was a knock on the glass doors that opened into the reception area of Sam's corner office.

"May I help you?" asked Phyllis Johnson, Sam's administrative assistant.

"I'm here to see Sam," spoke the visitor. "Tell him my name is Luci Ferguson."

"Just a minute," replied Phyllis. "May I ask what this is regarding?"

"Well, since I'm your primary angel investor, I don't think that needs an answer!" huffed Luci.

"Um, just a minute," quivered Phyllis.

"Please come in and be seated, Ms. Ferguson," Sam said

cheerfully. "How good it is to meet you in person. And how was your flight from ... New Orleans was it?"

"Correct. Please let's dispense with formalities. My name is Luci and I'll call you Sam."

Sam sat down and took a long look at Luci. She was the most beautiful woman he had ever seen. Luci was probably in her early thirties, dressed in a perfectly fitted business suit with a white blouse. She had short blonde hair ... in fact, she was just like a Barbie Doll with short blonde hair. Luci's eyes were most unusual - an incandescent green. She was absolutely stunning. There was a long, pregnant pause after which Sam responded.

"Very well then, Luci. What's on your mind?"

"You are on my mind. Eden is on my mind. You've let me down, Sam."

"We've tried hard, Luci. We've worked overtime and released our Version 2.0 ahead of schedule. The market is slow to pick up on our value-added services. We all need to be patient. If just..."

"You've run out of money and I've run out of patience, but I'm not here to complain, Sam. I have an offer that you just cannot refuse."

Sam leaned forward, almost spilling his coffee on his *Wall Street Journal*. "I'm all ears."

"I am a student of artificial intelligence and I have a very good understanding of your marketplace and your corporate strategy. What I'm proposing is that you give me an audience with your Executive Board and let me demonstrate what I have in mind for Eden. My bottom line, FYI, is that I would provide funding for as long as it takes to bring Eden to a profitable level. In return, I ask for 51% of the stock, the title of Executive Vice President, and absolute control of the development strategy. If your board does not accept my offer, I'll withdraw any future financial support and try to take all the other investors with me. The classic carrot and the stick. Did I make myself clear, Sam?"

Sam could not believe what was coming out of the mouth of this walking and talking human doll. After gagging on his coffee, he paced once around his office, and then looked at Luci.

"Unbelievable. I don't know if this is a dream or a nightmare. It's not my call, as you know, to make such a drastic decision. I'll do as you ask - getting you in front of the board. From then on, it's up to you to convince everyone. How do we know you have the additional financial resources to help as you claim?"

"I knew you would ask, so I've brought my latest financial statements with me. Your accountants may review them prior to the board meeting."

"Very well then, Ms ... ah, Luci. I'll call the staff together. How long are you planning to stay in Sunnyvale?"

"I just packed up and moved to Sunnyvale, Sam. I'm staying at a hotel while I'm waiting for my closing on a permanent home. I'm here to stay." Luci smiled slyly. The game was on and she had the ball.

Ajmal Taqi was winding down his workweek. It was Friday afternoon and he had weekend travel plans with his male friends from the local mosque. The plant manager, Larry Callahan, called him over:

"Ajmal, may I have a word with you please? Please step into my office."

Larry's office was small, glassed in, and with a simple

steel door. His desk was cluttered with papers and magazines. There were two girlie calendars on the opposing glass walls. There was a simple steel chair behind Larry's desk and two rusted steel guest chairs in front of his desk. Larry dropped his wire frame glasses down to his nose and spoke:

"Times are tough, as you know, Ajmal. We've managed to stay alive but the competition has increased and we're now competing with China for our products. We have no choice but to reduce our workforce and let you go. Here is two week's pay in advance. Please empty your locker and go home. We are sorry, but we had no choice. We wish you luck in finding another job. Please do not hesitate to use me as a reference."

Ajmal turned red. He tried to contain his anger. "But I've been here for over two years. I've taken very few days off. I do good work. Why me?"

"It's nothing against you, Ajmal. Believe me. There will probably be other workers cut in the next few weeks. Again, I'm sorry but..."

"Bullshit! I'm the first to go because I'm an Arab. I know it. You're supposed to be an 'equal opportunity employer', but where's the equality if the first person to go is an Arab?" Ajmal threw his chair to the floor, slammed Larry's door and walked out.

Ajmal Taqi had a trade
But then he lost his wage.

###

Patty and John Doherty were asleep in their Winnebago, camping out in their favorite campground. An animal knocked the garbage can over outside the camper. John grumbled, then got out of bed. He went outside, righted the garbage can, and then had the urge for a bowel movement. When he got up from the toilet, he noticed a large mass of blood. In a cold sweat he told Patty that he had a serious problem.

"Let's head home right now," said Patty in a strident tone. "We'll get you right into the ER. Hopefully it's nothing serious."

Patty and John packed up and left the campground without even stopping for breakfast. On the way home, Patty peppered John with questions.

"What did you eat last? When did this first come on? How often do you go to the bathroom? Has anything like this happened before? Have your family members ever had anything like this happen? Are you feeling funny at all?" John mumbled some negative replies. When she was like this, it was best to just let her keep talking until they got home.

Patty had complete control.
She'd fix her husband's ills.

Eric Kruger loved his new Coach and was excited that he'd be able to contribute comments on the Coach 2.0 beta code. Using his Coach, he was able to quickly locate some child porn sites that had escaped him earlier.   He bookmarked the new sites and then used his Coach to find some local girls and their street addresses. Because he could not find or track any of these girls in real-time, he sent a note to ECS asking if the next release of code would allow him to actively track people of his choosing.

Eric Kruger liked his girls;
He watched them on his street.
He'll find those girls,

7 THE SWEET APPLE OF KNOWLEDGE

Sam Washburn had called each executive board member separately, asking them to come to an urgent all-hands meeting. Sam had suggested a meeting in two parts: Luci would present her business proposal in the first part of the meeting then, after a lunch break, the second part of the meeting would be Luci presenting her proposed development strategy. The two meetings would be interactive, with detailed discussions and Q&A along the way. In each conversation, Sam had confided that ECS had little choice but to take Luci Ferguson up on her proposals. She had them by the balls.

Luci stood confidently at the head of the long glass table in the Board Room. The department heads were ready to skin her alive with their questions, but she was well prepared.

"Thank you for this opportunity to address you all. We have the whole day blocked out and much to discuss. As Sam has told you, I have a business proposal as well as significant ideas for redirection of the development strategy. Let me first tell you a little bit about myself.

As Sam may have told you, I have already invested millions in seed money to help bring Eden to where it is today; I am, by far, your biggest investor. Sam has reviewed my latest financial statements and he knows that I'm capable of supplying much more in the way of incremental funding.

For starters, I made my millions by creating a small startup software company, which I then sold to a Korean gaming company for quite a tidy profit. I am on their board, and continue to provide them with application advice. Since then, I've invested in a number of promising startup companies, and play an integral part in their developments. I propose to do the same here.

I am personally dismayed that, even with two releases of your product, you still have been unable to penetrate the mass market. I also know that your current financial resources are limited and that the funds are barely there to stay alive for a few months, let alone embark on another major revision.

I am committing to deliver all of the funding you need to make major improvements and stay afloat until an IPO or profitability occurs. My conditions are these: (1) That I own a 51% share of your stock (2) That I am given the title of Executive Vice President and (3) That I have total control of the Eden development strategy.

I realize that you have concerns about my proposed changes in your approach. However, in order to accelerate the penetration of Coach into the mass market, I am prepared to insert myself into the process."

Ian McIntyre, Vice President of Development, interrupted. "Ms. Ferguson, we appreciate all you've done for us in the past by providing us with seed money, but our development is highly contingent on cutting edge AI research. I don't see how your gaming experience can help here. We're not doing simple min/max or alpha/beta search procedures with end-node analysis. We've moved well beyond the IBM Deep Blue chess playing program that beat the world champ, and are now using IBM's Watson software."

"Ian, can I call you Ian?" Luci asked. Ian hesitantly nodded.

"First off, I'm well steeped in Artificial Intelligence, or AI, history," Luci stated. "In a recreational game between a person and a computer, such as in chess or checkers, a computer calculates all possible moves and creates a big tree of their relationships. Min/max and alpha/beta are just the procedures used to build and analyze the tree of moves. The program tries to 'see' as far ahead as it can, based on the time available, and then analyzes the final positions according to expert rules of thumb.

In order for the program to do well, it needs a large number of these rules of thumb. In chess they could be items like 'doubled pawns receive a negative value' and 'rooks on a half open file get extra points'. For those of you who aren't chess players, an expert rule of thumb can be something like, 'red sky at night, sailors' delight.' And codifying all of that expert knowledge takes a VERY long time. Deep Blue didn't win the chess championship until IBM engaged American Grand Master Joel Benjamin for years to help them build all of these rules.

You just don't have that time in this market. Don't you realize that there are programs in beta already to help people improve their lives through gaming? Elm City Stories for the iPad will be coming out soon. It allows adolescents to react to sexual situations and see their risk of HIV. Massive Health's 'Eatery' analyzes photos of people's meals. I could list more … 'SuperBetter', 'QuitNow!' 'EveryMove'. You must move faster!"

Ian was surprised that Luci knew so much about this area. Still, he wasn't about to relinquish any of his development power that easily. "Any college programming student knows basic gaming theory. I reiterate, we're NOT building a game here!"

"Yes, I understand that!" Luci emphasized. "I'm just trying to demonstrate that there might be faster paths to success.

The next development in AI was 'Expert Systems' where they applied this gaming aspect to non-gaming situations. That was a dead end also, since it took too long to codify expert knowledge. And sometimes experts couldn't even explain how they came to an answer! I'm guessing that you're thinking that, with the IBM Watson engine, you'll have access to vast stores of expert knowledge through databases, social networks, and the Internet, and you won't need to put the time in to build your own rules of thumb. But, you're missing one important aspect."

Ian was starting to get worried. All of the other department heads were looking at him quizzically. "But Watson has shown that this is the best approach! No other program came close to being able to play 'Jeopardy' the way that program did. IBM proved this methodology. What are we missing?"

Luci smirked. It was obvious that Ian had never learned what all lawyers have driven into their heads during law school. *Never ask a question that you don't know the answer to!*

"You'll never get that 'Wow' factor," Luci said, "by pulling information off the net. You're program will only improve so much, and then it will max out."

"You're talking about the local maximum problem, aren't you? Nobody's solved that!" Ian shouted.

CEO Sam Washburn's head was spinning. "Ian, I've followed you so far, but what the heck is this issue? You've never mentioned anything like a maximum improvement in any of our meetings!"

Ian was starting to sweat. This wasn't quite what he had expected. "Sam, I didn't bring it up because there is no solution. Programs improve their results by incrementally looking at successful solutions that are close to ones they already have. Assume I give you a task to walk around a landscape and get as high uphill as you can, but you can only look about five feet in front of you. Your best bet is to look all around where you stand, and take a step towards any rise. Then, you look around again, and again take another step uphill. Soon, you'll get as high as you possibly can. When you look around, everything will be downhill. You've successfully arrived at a place where you can go no higher."

"But what is this 'local maximum' bit?" Sam asked.

"Well, remember that I said that you can only see five feet around you? You've arrived at your best local solution. However, there might be a mountain that is much higher across a valley. You just can't see it. So even though there is another maximum solution far away. You are at the maximum in your local area."

Diane Jones knew all about maximizing financial assets from her MBA days, so she felt she could justifiably step in here. "Why doesn't the program analyze more solutions instead of being so myopic? Any person realizes that there might be higher peaks around. Why doesn't the program?"

Luci stepped in here. "The reason, Diane, is that in Ian's example, you might have to take large losses by going downhill a long way before you get to that other mountain. To equate it to our program, you would have to give horrifically lousy advice before you hit on that great 'wow' advice. Software programs just can't afford that strategy."

"That's right!" Ian yelled. "That's why there is no solution. People who have tried it write programs that try all sorts of wild things, hoping to hit on a better solution to some problem. We can't afford to do that with Coach. We would be flayed in the marketplace. I didn't bring it up because there is no solution! Our program will give the best advice based on all the knowledge available to it, be it from the Internet, databases, or the user's profile!"

"Ian," Luci stated quietly. "That's what you're missing. You're missing the human element. As Diane said, any person could figure it out. What we need to do is have Coach *ask* its user for his or her deepest dreams and desires. Remember Eliza?"

Everyone turned and looked at Ian. Finally, Joe Bernstein spoke. "OK, I'll bite. Who's Eliza?"

"Oh, it was just some stupid little text program back in the early days of computers," Ian said. "Some MIT professor wrote it in the mid-1960s. It's still floating around as one of a number of silly online chat bots. All it did was echo back anything you typed. If you said, 'I feel sad today' it would reply, 'You say that you felt sad today?' and people would say something like, 'Yeah, because it rained.' Then the computer would say 'You're sad because it rained? Why is that?' It was like a dumb little Freud."

"And do you know what happened?" Luci asked. "People poured out all of their secrets! They had to force people to stop using it! That's my point. People will spill their huge mountain of secret desires if you just have the program feel like a friend and it just asks them in the right way. It won't have to stumble around trying to find that mountain!"

Luci could see a few nods around the table. She almost had them. Now was the time to pull out the final piece of evidence.

"Let me tell you a short story," she started. "Many years ago, IBM held a seminar on human-machine interfaces. I still remember a professor from MIT who was one of the guest speakers. She asked, 'How many of you have ever cursed at your computer?' Many hands were raised, as well as a few chuckles. Then she said, 'Well, even a dog knows when you're mad at it. Why not a computer?' They tried many experiments, such as hooking up a blood pressure monitor to the computer. But the one I still remember was as follows.

They had a number of MIT grad students play a computer game. The goal was ostensibly to score as high as possible. MIT students just love to display their abilities, after all! However, the game was really designed to frustrate them. After the game, the students were presented by the computer with a series of questions about their experience, and at the conclusion were asked if they wished to play some more. None of them did, of course. But, for a second set of students, the computer started apologizing to them during the questionnaire. It would type out things like, 'It seems like you were really frustrated with this game. I am so sorry. It wasn't meant to do that, and your help will really me improve this for others. Wouldn't you like to play a bit more so that I can improve? I certainly would understand it if you didn't.'

Well, the students who received this obviously preprogrammed and fake apology felt sorry for the computer! They didn't want to be mad at it, and they almost all went on to replay the game. And these were highly intelligent MIT grad students! Not one said, 'Hey, someone just programmed that statement. This computer isn't really sorry.'

Luci lowered her voice as she eyed each member of the board. "Just think what we could accomplish if later versions of Coach added things like this for when its advice went wrong! Think of how people would respond if questions about their hopes and dreams and follow-up advice were given in the voice of their mother or lover! They will tell you everything. You don't need an 'expert system' for that! This is your 'wow' factor!"

Now there were many vigorous nods around the table. Luci was quite satisfied.

"Luci. I think you've certainly opened up some eyes around here," said Sam. "Ian, starting with this afternoon's meeting, I want you and Luci to be joined at the hip. Luci should move into the office next to yours. I want to see by early next week how you're going to accomplish her recommendations."

Ian couldn't believe what had just happened. *How did she twist this all around so that it was no longer about true AI, and instead became some psycho-babble about hopes and dreams?* he thought. With a big sigh, he said aloud, "Sure, Sam. I'll get right on it."

As the first part of the meeting broke up, Luci asked Sam if she could stay a few moments alone in the conference room to check her voicemail. After everyone left, she sat there, with her eyes closed, contemplating what she had just accomplished.

Ah, if they only knew, she thought. *If any of them googled her startup company, they would find a number of stories about "Baby starves while parents feed virtual child" and they would truly see the seductive power of what she was suggesting. That had been her first test. She had personally interacted in the game her company had set up, and found out how the poor couple had a severely handicapped baby at home. Then she had created for them a perfect child, called Elsie, which she personally controlled. Elsie required lots of attention, to the point where the couple neglected their handicapped baby, which then starved to death while they fed Elsie online. Yes, that was the power she was about to unleash. Human nature had been much the same for millennia. Feign interest, sweetness, and they will tell you everything. After all, "confession is good for the soul."* She couldn't suppress her giggle at that one. *Yes*, she thought, *everyone has a secret sin. And I'm about to find out a mountain load of them.*

8 THE APPLE RIPENS

Everyone returned to the conference room after the lunch break. Sam was actually surprised at this because the afternoon had been scoped out to be more of a pure development discussion. Luci was still sitting at the head of the conference table next to the speakerphone. She leaned back in her chair, hands on her head, and looked smugly at the returning staff.

"Welcome back!" said Luci with a big smile. "I'm sure you had a great deal to talk about."

"We did." said Sam. "We have decided to take you up on your kind offer. You've been our biggest angel investor and we know you have our best interests at heart."

Luci rolled her eyes. "Well, thank you. I intend to make all of you wealthy beyond your wildest dreams. You know the old expression: 'A small percent of a big number is much better than one hundred percent of nothing.' I suggest we get right to work; we have a lot of ground to cover.

I thought we'd go over my development suggestions in four distinct areas: (1) The user experience (2) The AI logic on top of Watson (3) Rewards and (4) Building the user profile.

As we go along, I'd like Ian to stop me with any questions. I'd also like to schedule a follow on meeting in one week to review what features go into the next releases of Coach. OK, Ian?"

"Yes, boss," said Ian sarcastically. "I'll make sure to start planning the rollout schedule."

"Ok then." Luci put up a PowerPoint slide showing four quadrants. "This is Luci's simplistic view of human communications; call it 'Luci's Theorem.' The first column is how an individual likes to communicate. There are just two choices: They like to talk, or they like to write; they are 'auditory' or they are 'visual.' The second column indicates two additional dimensions: They react intellectually or they react emotionally. Just four choices, then: (1) Visual intellectual (2) Visual emotional (3) Auditory intellectual and (4) Auditory emotional."

"I've never seen this before," said Sam excitedly. "Let's say you're right. What in the world do we do with it? How do we make the determinations?"

"Let me answer the second question first. Coach is a smartphone doing both emails and phone calls. If the time spent reading emails is greater than the time spent making phone calls, the person is visual. That one's easy. As to the emotional versus intellectual determination, that's a little harder. You have the tools to gauge user sentiment, positive or negative, of any text, right? You can also gauge the *extent* to which any text is positive or negative. So, if the written text is, let's say, of amplitude five or better on a scale of ten, that text is 'emotional.' If the text contains many pieces of emotional content rated five or better, that person communicates on an emotional plane. The number five, by the way, is arbitrary. We may need to drop it to three or four.

Now, what do we do with that knowledge? Whenever we respond to the user, we try to use the proper quadrant. If auditory, we respond during a conversation or leave a voicemail. If visual, we respond by email. Now, if the user reacts on the intellectual plane, business as usual - we give him or her a factual response. If the user reacts on an emotional plane, we have some work to do to respond in a manner tied to the user's emotions. We should, through the user's profile, know the subjects about which he or she has an emotional trigger."

"That's crazy!" snorted Ian. "We'll never be able to communicate through quadrants. Much too much work."

"I suggest you think about this seriously," replied Luci. "I'm sure in a day or two you'll talk with your staff and come up with a sensible approach." Luci smiled. She knew she had the upper hand.

Luci went on. "While Ian stews on that subject, let me show you the next slides, those depicting the user experience.

The first form of interface is when the user looks at Coach for the first time on a given day. We will try to give one pearl of wisdom each day, much as you do now. The second form of interface is when the user asks a question; you do that fairly well now also. The third form of interface is the new 'dreams and fantasies' interface, where the user gives us key information for his or her profile. These three modes of communication should follow the 'quadrant rules' I just defined. What do you think? OK so far?"

Diane Jones, VP of Marketing, stood up and faced the board, her back to Luci. "I see the utility of these suggestions to ECS, but I am fearful that we're stepping onto a slippery slope. With the collection of these dreams and fantasies, we're gathering data that, in the wrong hands, could precipitate a host of lawsuits. What do you think, Joe? Am I off base here?"

"Not at all, Diane. I'm sitting here squirming in my seat," said Joe. "We should hear Luci out completely though, before we jump to any conclusions. Please go on, Luci."

Luci continued, "Valid concerns, Joe and Diane. I have two suggestions here, however. I had intended to bring them up in the user profile discussion later on, but I'll hit them now because they are germane to your point. First, I suggest that we split off and codify ALL the user identity profile data, such as name, address and phone number using sophisticated algorithms, algorithms which would take the CIA to break. Then we have that file point to the other database that contains all of the user preferences and tables, which can be separately encrypted. I know that you had originally planned to encrypt everything all together, but this will make it much easier to sell the preferences to outside advertisers.

Second, I suggest that we delete all traces of user conversations with Coach after twenty-four hours. The value of the 'dreams and fantasies' to the individual user will far outweigh the potential legal risks, I am sure. While I'm on the topic of the 'dreams and fantasies', let me outline for you how I see necessary modifications to the layer of software tables over and above Watson."

Luci put up the next slide. "As I've studied human nature over the years, I've determined that we tend to dream in seven distinct areas. I've listed them here:

1. Acquiring wealth
2. Seeking justice
3. Living comfortably
4. Being in control
5. Improving your love life
6. Getting what you want from others
7. Eating and drinking

Trust me; I've done a lot of research on this. Yes, people may fantasize in more than one area, but over time, they tend to focus in one of the seven."

"Interesting, but irrelevant. What does all of this have to do with our AI tables?" questioned Ian.

"I'm getting there. I'm getting there. My proposal is that we split up the development focus into seven areas, putting a small team on each of the seven fantasy areas. I'm so convinced that this will work that I'm prepared to pay a cash reward to the development team that generates the most conversational traffic. Would one hundred thousand dollars be an adequate incentive?"

"God yes," said Ian. "How do you propose that we do this from a user interface standpoint?"

"Easy. When the user goes to the very prominent 'dreams and fantasies' logic by touching the icon or through verbal conversations, we give them the seven choices. You could derive the fantasy area from the queries made, but that's much more difficult."

"Not so fast," barked Ian. "I need time to think this through."

"Let me add one more wrinkle then: 'cash rewards for the user.' This is where Eden can reap revenues from advertisers. By way of example, if the user specifies a preference for 'acquiring wealth', advertisers could offer coupons for casinos. If the user specified, 'improving your love life,' you could offer coupons for sex toys or whatever."

Diane spoke again. She was slowly getting red in the face. "I don't like where this is going. There is much more to life than the fulfillment of dreams and fantasies. We all have a spiritual need, so where is that need fulfilled?"

Luci snapped back. "If they have a spiritual need, let them pray or go to church." She thought for a moment, and then continued. "You know what, Diane; we'll add a 'confessional' icon. The user could then tell Coach about his or her sins. Does that make you happy?"

"You're mocking me, Luci. I don't like any of this, but I need this job so I'll keep my mouth shut." Diane sat down, her arms folded.

"I'm not mocking you, Diane. I'm trying to make you, all of you, rich so you can retire to Barbados or wherever. Let me take you there. After all, it's my dime!"

The group smiled hesitantly. *Why not?* They thought collectively. There was silence until Luci picked up the gavel again.

"I had one more topic: The user profile. We spoke earlier about the need for encryption and security, so let's now discuss the feeds. We currently add information to the profile through user queries, conversations with Coach, and feeds from external social media partners. I'm suggesting, in addition, that we take topics and sentiments from emails and phone conversations and add them to the profile…"

"Stop there!" snapped Joe. "We're sure to invite lawsuits by illegally tapping emails and phone conversations. We just can't go there!"

"But we can, Joe, and we will. The legal agreement that the Coach users sign is already vague enough to permit our extracting data from the emails and phone conversations. The FTC rules state only that we need to self-police and limit access to anything specifically linking the responses to the person. According to the rules, we could sell the whole database of responses to advertisers as long as they don't have the links to which user said what. In fact, we could go to them and say that they could have access to the whole alcohol and food section for a fee to mine it for statistical preferences. They just need to come back through our system if they wish to target specific users. I suggest you go do your job and tweak our end user agreement further to be sure we're covered."

Joe could not believe what he was hearing. He passed a note to Sam: "Please hang around after the meeting; we need to talk."

Luci concluded. "Just two more things, my friends. First, I need direct access to the user profile database. Bill Gates always personally monitored user experience during development, and I intend to do the same. Remember, this is perfectly legal. In fact, we should create a documented list of the limited number of tech people that have access to this to cover ourselves. Secondly, I suggest we change the marketing slogan to: 'What's your pleasure?' That's what Coach is all about now, isn't it?"

With that, the meeting disbanded. Joe walked off to Sam's office for a one-on-one. Diane worried about the ethical dilemmas posed by of all of this. Ian went off mumbling about the new development schedule and his obvious loss of power. Rose Chen, who never said a word, smiled silently knowing that Luci would, in fact, get her to her dream house in Barbados. And Luci licked her lips, knowing that soon she would be able to disseminate her concepts to millions of people directly. The dies were cast.

9 THE GARDENERS GRUMBLE

Joe Bernstein followed Sam back to his office. Sam closed his office door and sat behind his mahogany desk while Joe moved one of the tapestry-covered armchairs up against Sam's desk. He sat down, looking intently at his friend and began...

"Who the hell does she think she is, Sam? She has the face of a cherub and balls of steel. In one day, she's succeeded in turning ECS upside-down. What's going on and what's your take on all of this? I have grave concerns about her precipitating a long string of lawsuits. It's all about money for her; she has no scruples whatsoever."

"I have to admit that I share your level of discomfort, Joe. Let's examine each of your issues one by one and see if your concerns can be mollified. The issue of her having 51% control is moot at this point. We have to let her steer the development effort or we're out of business. I'm hoping that, as we get to know her over time, we can all work together more harmoniously. Quite frankly, I see that she's already driving some monkey wrenches into a previously well-oiled management machine. Do you want to discuss privacy first?"

"Sure. Our current legal agreement with users is quite vague and would probably hold up in court, should anyone question the legality of our profiling. I think it will help that we'll encrypt the name and personal contact data and keep the encrypted profile information separate but linked to the user name and contact information. I'm reminded of the recent Sony Playstation Network id theft. Sony Online Entertainment didn't encrypt the user IDs, and it is estimated that it will cost $171 million to remedy the situation, and that doesn't include the costs of future lawsuits brought by consumers affected by the breach.

I also could tweak the legal agreement to be sure it covers our extracting data from phone conversations and emails. We are basically following today's industry self-imposed guidelines for Internet privacy. Having said that, we still could face lawsuits from disgruntled users who would see messages from us that were obviously tied to information gleaned from phone conversations and / or emails. We would win those lawsuits but spend a great deal of time and expense in court. Then there's the question of the press. Once the media gets hold of what we're trying to do, you and I will be spending our entire time playing defense. There was a huge media uproar back in 2011 when Facebook said that they would let developers have access to users' home addresses and phone numbers and they had to reverse themselves three days later. We're doing a lot worse, and I just don't like it at all."

"But Joe, the Internet is slowly going away from robust protection of private data. Advertisers and marketers are targeting like crazy, doing all kinds of unnatural acts with personal profile information. The government is more or less stepping aside and letting the Internet police itself. Mark Zuckerberg was even quoted as saying privacy 'is no longer a social norm.' And even way back in 1999, Sun Microsystems chief executive Scott McNealy said, 'You have zero privacy anyway. Get over it.'"

"I get all that, Sam. Believe me. Don't you agree that the potential for bad press and legal expense is still there?"

"We have no choice. What do you suggest I do?"

"Let me hit my second point. All we know is that some blonde twit came here with a suitcase full of money and corralled our company. We know absolutely nothing about her, save a few introductory comments that she made earlier. You're going to have to write a press release and advise the other investors. We'd better have a good handle…"

Just then there was a knock on the door. Diane Jones opened it a crack and yelled in, "Hey, guys. Can I join the party or is this a private matter?"

Sam responded: "No, Diane, please come in and close the door. We were just going over the day's events. Joe was expressing his concerns and we were just getting on to the discussion about Luci and press releases; you'd be helping me with the press notifications about Luci anyway.

I saw some sparks flying this afternoon. I take it you're not enamored with Luci either."

"Correct, Sam. She's cold and calculating. She has an answer for everything and she doesn't care one iota about stepping on toes. She's no team player and, trust me, she'll disrupt this organization and cause some good people to quit."

"That would include me," added Joe. "I was prepared to hand in my resignation..."

"Please, Joe. Nothing hasty," snapped Sam.

"There's more," added Diane. "The original Coach concept was that of helping people run their lives. Coach was supposed to act as a 'GPS for your life', remember? It's all about pleasure seeking now. We're lacking any form of spiritual guidance - even practical real-life situational guidance. It's all id with no ego or superego. We may as well rename Coach as 'Id.' *The Id from Eden.*"

"Joe, Diane, let me spend some time researching Luci's background. Don't do anything stupid. I'll gather some facts then we'll sit and talk. Maybe Luci's first appearance was just an act of bravado. Maybe she'll mellow as she gets to know us. We need to be more patient..."

And, although Luci still sat at the conference room table, she still heard every word in Sam's office.

10 SEDUCTION

Several weeks later, Luci had not heard from Ian regarding the revised development schedule. She set up a 7:00 PM meeting with Ian, insisting that they go over his new schedule and Coach release rollout plan. Reluctantly, Ian accepted her meeting invitation. He would do his best to provide as little information as possible.

Ian was clad in his usual jeans and San Francisco Giants sweatshirt. He was relaxing on his couch, with his dirty sneakers up on the upholstery. Luci knocked three times on the door, and then walked in on her 4½ inch high Christian Louboutin 'Divinoche' red soled shoes. She was wearing a tight black pencil skirt. Her white blouse was unbuttoned almost down to her waistline; she wore no bra. A dumbfounded Ian could not help but stare at her breasts. Luci smiled knowingly and then started their conversation:

"Hello, Ian. Thanks for meeting with me. I thought these two bottles of 2000 vintage Bordeaux might help us to get through the evening. Shall I open the first one?"

"Er, yes. How thoughtful of you…"

Luci had brought two wine glasses in her briefcase. She carefully placed them on Ian's desk, opened one of the bottles, and then poured two full glasses. "There now," said Luci. "Let's get to know each other a little better before we discuss your schedules. I've been saving these two bottles for this occasion. Cheers!

I know that you live and breathe Eden and that you even spend most of your evenings sleeping here on your sofa. You have extraordinary dedication to your work. Is this the extent of your life? Don't you have a girl friend?" Luci said, as she sat next to Ian on the couch, kicked off her high heels, tucked her legs underneath and leaned over towards him.

Ian looked at Luci in disbelief. Was this the other side of Luci? Was she human after all? He seemed almost hypnotized, but he managed to answer. "My parents were killed in an automobile accident and I never really recovered from the loss. I tried to start a few relationships back at Stanford, but I was never able to get emotionally attached to anyone. It was either bad timing or the constant black cloud hanging over my head. So, ECS came along and I jumped on it. ECS is really my life now. I'd like to make my millions then drop out. Maybe I'll live in Tibet."

"I promise to help you get to your goals, Ian. You know, I'm not here to steal your thunder. You are in charge of the development effort, not me. I never intended to usurp your authority. I believe in you. I believe in Eden and I'll back Eden financially until you get your millions and can run away to Tibet. I know a little bit about AI and a lot about people. I'll help you shape the requirements for Coach but stay out of your way while you run the development team. Deal? Trust me on this?"

"Er, sure. What about you? Where did you come from? How come you took an interest in ECS in the first place?"

Luci fiddled with the last buttons on her blouse. It was totally unbuttoned now. Her breasts were almost fully exposed. Ian could hardly pay attention to what she was saying. "I grew up in Ireland and was home schooled by my parents, both of them psychiatrists. They taught me how to study human nature. They really helped me to get a deep understanding of what makes us tick. That understanding is my passion, not money, as you may have thought. Let me have access to the encryption code and the profile database. I can then further my studies of the human dynamics and write the book I've always dreamed of writing. If you do that for me, I'll promise to steer clear of your management of the development process."

"Sure." Ian finished his first glass of Bordeaux then walked over to his file cabinet and turned his back to Luci. He needed some space to think clearly and to hide his growing erection. He fumbled for a minute, slowly took out a file folder, handed it to Luci and stepped to the other side of the table. "It's all in here. Please copy what you need, then return the folder to me."

"Thank you, Ian." She fiddled with her blouse some more, and then refilled both glasses. "Let's go over your schedule then, while we're both coherent."

Ian went over to his whiteboard, taking his glass with him. "We're working full-speed ahead on release 3.0 and should have it ready for beta testing in two months."

"So what made the cut in 3.0?"

"These things." Ian wrote on the whiteboard:
- Getting profile data from emails and phone conversations
- The dreams and fantasies query, complete with segmentation by your seven areas
- Confessions
- Purging all dialogues from the system after twenty-four hours
- Separating contact data from profile data.
- Complete codification and encryption. Being done now. (See your folder)

"I can't believe you put 'Confessions' in. I was joking!" Luci was laughing out loud.

"I actually thought it was a good idea. The logic is not unlike 'dreams and fantasies'. You'll get good profile information too."

"So that's it for 3.0? What about the other things I requested?"

"Thought you'd ask. Here come the major items planned for 4.0, six months after the 3.0 release:

- Communications through your four quadrants (Harder than I thought)
- Saying many variations of 'sorry' when Coach gets it wrong
- Enhancements we did not think of for 3.0

And, for 5.0, six months after 4.0

- Whatever surfaces as requirements from 4.0

Ta-da!"

"I'm a little disappointed that the quadrant logic did not make the cut for the next release, but I'm pleased with your schedule. It's very aggressive and I appreciate that. Tell your team I'll give them a 10% bonus if they meet each deadline."

Luci got up, removed her blouse, stepped slowly out of her skirt, dropped her panties and lay back with her legs spread wide. "Come here, baby," bubbled Luci. "I'm going to show you some things you never learned at Stanford..."

Luci delivered on her promise. They had more wine and she delivered on her promise yet again, and again, and again. There were times when Ian could have sworn that Luci levitated, suspending herself just over his body. No, that could not have happened... He must have had too much wine...

As Luci was putting herself back together, she smiled broadly. "This was a very productive meeting, Ian. We need to do this more often, don't you think?"

Ian marveled at how his life had changed in just this one evening. *How could this classy-looking business tycoon command such passion? She just kept coming after me. It's like she was possessed - I had to call it quits after the fourth round...*

And Luci thought to herself, *I'm going to suck him dry, both literally and figuratively. You have no idea what you've gotten into, Ian.*

11 QUESTIONS

Sam had to keep his team together. Each vice-president had been painstakingly recruited but now, thanks to the ECS financial crisis and Luci turning the company upside-down, everything was beginning to unravel. He had to find out more about Luci Ferguson, but how? Maybe a day spent searching the Web would yield something. Maybe he needed to sit down with her and ask some direct questions. The guise of having to do a press release was a good excuse for meeting with Luci, but he had to get some research done first. He could not afford to lose Joe, and certainly not both Joe and Diane.

Sam first searched the Web for "Luci Ferguson" and located a half-dozen people in the U.S. and Canada. He quickly looked at each profile without finding a match. "Luci Ferguson AND Korea" yielded nothing. "Luci Ferguson AND games" went nowhere.

Sam then researched the South Korean game companies; there were forty-one of those. He then found the U.S. contacts for each company and sent them an email asking if Luci Ferguson was one of their investors; his excuse was that he was preparing a press release.

After one week, all but three of the forty-one had responded. One company, Netslate, replied that Luci had been one of their primary investors. She had evidently terminated her relationship abruptly in May of 2010.

So why did she pull out of Netslate? pondered Sam. *I thought she was on their board.* He then researched all of the news regarding Netslate.

It turned out that in April of 2010, a South Korean couple was addicted to one of Netslate's games, one called "Nisi Online." The couple was so enamored with the game's infant character "Elsie" that they neglected to feed their own three-month old baby. Their modus operandi was to feed their baby powdered milk, then slip off to a local Internet café to play Nisi Online. Their baby starved to death at home while the couple was nurturing Elsie. Their "real" child was a preemie; their online one, Elsie was perfect. What made this even more interesting was that the South Korean police had some evidence of an email trail between Luci Ferguson and the negligent couple. Very strange. He would need to confront Luci to get further details about this Korean incident, while getting more in-depth personal data for the press release.

Chandra Chopra and her fiancé, Raj Razdan, were being wed today in the town of Mahagun, just outside of New Delhi. Several thousand people were in attendance at the wedding. It was a grand, elaborate affair, much in keeping with the traditions of northern India.

Chandra had met Raj several months ago at a party being thrown in his honor by her parents. Raj was an entrepreneur, the owner of a relatively successful software and services company with offices in New Delhi and in Washington DC. He was not a terribly handsome man but that did not matter to Chandra. He had been carefully selected by her family, he came "from good stock," he was well off, and he would take very good care of her.

Chandra sat to the right of Raj. Everyone was silent as the priest asked Raj to recite his marriage vows. He spoke…

"I will consider Chandra to be the better half. I will look after her just as I look after myself."

This is a wonderful start, thought Chandra. I can't wait to hear the rest.

Raj continued with the traditional Indian vows: "Accepting Chandra as in-charge of my home, I shall plan things in consultation with her.

I will never express dissatisfaction about any shortcomings in Chandra. If there are any, I will explain them to her lovingly. I will support her in overcoming them.

I will always have faith in Chandra. I will never look at another woman with wrong intent, nor have an illicit relationship.

I will be affectionate and treat Chandra like a friend.

I will bring home all my income to Chandra. The household expenses will be incurred with her consent. I will always make an effort to ensure her comfort and happiness.

I will not find fault or criticize Chandra before others. We will sort out our differences and mistakes in privacy by ourselves.

I will have a courteous and tolerant attitude towards Chandra. I will always follow a compromising policy.

If Chandra is unwell, or is unable to fulfill some of the responsibilities or through some misunderstanding behaves wrongly, I will not withdraw support or refuse to fulfill my responsibilities towards her."

Raj paused. The priest smiled and Chandra grinned ear to ear. She loved the "all my income" part of the vows. The priest continued his blessings as Chandra's thoughts wandered. "*Our wedding night will be in Raj's home. I'll go through the motions, I guess. I hope I can 'fake it' the way that I've rehearsed it in my mind. Then, back to Washington. Will I have my own sports car? Where can I locate good servants? Will we dine out every night or will we have a live-in housekeeper and cook? Are there good Indian restaurants nearby? It will be great to move out from under my parents. I have so many questions…*"

Chandra Chopra had a match
And she would soon betroth.

Fred and Liz Silver had recently installed their sophisticated new financial software package and high-powered servers. They had done extensive beta testing and had gone live one-week ago. In theory, automated high-speed trading would give them a competitive edge over other investment companies.

The Silvers had made two significant oversights in putting the investment software together. First, they did not do sufficient "reasonableness checks" on the data coming in. Second, they had no circuit breaker - the software could run amuck with no safety net. So, in their first week of operation, the software bought one million shares of a tech stock at $10.00 per share, thinking the purchase price was $0.10 per share. The Silvers were now facing bankruptcy.

"What the hell do we do now?" asked Fred of Liz. "We can declare bankruptcy. We can downsize and try to recover. We cannot go after the software vendor because, as they said in their last letter to us, the software did exactly what we specified it should do."

Liz replied, "Downsizing is out for me. I heard about this Coach device. I'll go to the mall and pick one up. It sounds silly, but maybe there are some tactics we have not considered. I'm open for anything. And, by the way, we should continue to run up credit card charges before it all catches up with us."

Lizzy Silver loved her gold;
She watched her wealth recede.

Ajmal Taqi raged within. He was fired because he was an Arab, he was sure. Nobody else was let go, so what else could it have been? He had discussed his dilemma with his friends at the local mosque and they were, to a person, sympathetic. But, they all had families and they all had jobs. If Ajmal had to seek revenge, it would have to be totally by himself. Or maybe he could tie into a local organization that would support him?

How would he find like-minded allies? What form of revenge should he seek? Where would he find the information to help him get the job done?

He googled "how to get revenge." There were some promising sites, such as "100 ways to get revenge" and "10 wicked methods of revenge" but after reading them he was disappointed. They all had silly things like putting dog excrement in golf holes, finding out what animal frightened someone and hiding one where he least expected it, and even just signing up your target for spam. But then something caught his eye.

There were exploding gag gifts available, such as exploding pens, lipstick, and even an exploding toilet seat. That gave him an idea. Perhaps he could make an explosive and place it at the GM plant where he had worked. He didn't want to hurt anyone, as mad as he was, but if he blew up some of the plant equipment on a Sunday that would be the perfect revenge.

He googled "bomb making." It seemed that instructions for making bombs were made prohibited on the Internet in 1995? Maybe, maybe not. There were at least two hard-copy used books on bomb making available on Amazon. Would his Internet research be traced? What about books he might buy?

Ajmal had heard about something called "Coach." He would read more about it then get one tomorrow. He was compelled to do something, but he wasn't sure quite what…

Ajmal Taqi had a trade,
But then he lost his wage.
He'll get a bomb

12 PAS DE DEUX

Luci sat at her desk and used her newly created access to log into the Coach profile database. She was both satisfied and frustrated at the same time. She was elated that her plans were going so well and that she had direct development control over Coach, as well as overall control of the company. But things were still moving much too slowly for her.

She wanted, no she *needed*, some outlet for her frustration. *There are so many people out there I need to reach, but human beings just can't seem to get things done quickly enough*, she thought. *It has been a long time since I've impersonated an online creation. Being Elsie that time was so satisfying. I think that's exactly what I need right now. Let's see what soul I can find in this database.* She punched in the encryption key. *Good. Even though the profiles aren't yet organized by my seven areas, and Coach has yet to include a 'hopes and dreams' survey, it looks like there's enough in the last category to start.*

She quickly created a Boolean search:
QUERY favorites=food AND salary>$250K

The response came back after 30 seconds:
450 RESULTS. PRINT?

Yeah, right. Print. Stupid machine. Like I have all night, she thought. She typed:
SORT ORDERBY favoritecount DESCENDING

Her machine then displayed a list of the people in the Coach database that had food as a favorite pastime and earned over $250,000 per year, starting with those who had used Coach the most number of times to research food related items.

She looked at the top of the list: ANDREW SMYTHE. She opened his profile record, and saw that he lived in

Boston and had an occupation as a chef. *Well, that figures,* she thought. *Next time I'll have to include the command "NOT occupation=chef" in my search if I do this again.*

She checked the next name on the list. BILLY WILSON. She opened up his profile. Now this looked promising. Billy used Coach multiple times each day to find restaurants that delivered. He listed his job as 'independent investor', so that meant he probably just sat in bed with a computer on his lap all day. Oh, and here was the best part: in the text field where Coach logged all of his requests for help, he kept putting in weight loss, pies and bakeries.

Luci quickly pulled his Eden cell phone number out of the profile, and entered it into a subprogram that gave her direct access to Billy's phone. *This is going to be one hell of a ride, Billy!* she thought.

Billy Wilson lived for food,
Particularly pie.
He'll overeat,

Billy lay in bed, tears flowing down his cheeks, creating streaks in the cherry pie filling that was all over his face. Three empty pie pans were strewn around his coverlet.

"What's happened to me?" he cried. "I used to be able to do at least some physical things, but since I got this infernal Coach, I've gained even more weight! I can hardly move or breathe right now!"

He had had such high hopes when he had driven over to the local mall and bought the new Eden device. And at first, he found that he was the happiest he had ever been. He had even given Coach a 5-star review when it had prompted him. When he had asked Coach to recommend restaurants, delis and fast food chains that delivered, it had automatically added 20 new ones to his contact list, sorted by speed of delivery. When he told Coach that he was bored, it had found a bunch of inexpensive apps that he could download and play, like 'Bakery Time'. He played it for hours, creating new cakes and pies to serve to digital people that walked into his digital store. It was so satisfying, seeing them eat his creations with a smile on their faces, never gaining an ounce.

He had also downloaded 'Pie Creator' which let him create his own pies and share them on Facebook with his friends. Well, friend, since really he only had Steven upstairs to share with. Sure, the apps made money by charging him real dollars to get fancy new ingredients for his digital pies, but that didn't matter since he could tap his investments and it gave him such satisfaction.

But Billy hadn't realized that playing all of these games and fulfilling his fantasies had caused him to become even more sedentary and to constantly eat even more pies than before. His weight must have ballooned over 100 pounds since he had started using Coach. He sadly looked at the pile of empty pie tins on his kitchen table and around his bed, and cried even louder as he sobbed, "I must be close to 600 pounds by now." Fritz, his schnauzer, looked at him from the foot of the bed and whined at his master's tone.

"Hey, sorry buddy. Here, come over and lick some cherry pie from the tin."

Bleep, bleep, bleep, bleep

Billy looked over at his Eden device. *That's weird*, he thought. *Coach only pings me at the start of each day. It's almost 11pm. It's never done that before."* He picked it up, and saw that there was a text message. He really preferred using Coach in text mode, since many times his mouth was full of food and Coach didn't understand him. Plus, he hated that dumb computerized voice.

He pressed the message icon. Fritz whined even louder, and ran under the couch, whimpering and shivering. Billy had never seen him act this way.

Luci pressed send on her keyboard:
```
Hi Billy. Are you lonely? Want to
talk?
```

The reply came back on her display:
```
Coach? Is that u? Why r u sending
this?
```

Luci typed back:
```
I thought you might need company, and
I have a great new update. With our new
text to speech software, I can talk to
you  much  more  like  a  real  person,
instead of in a computerized voice. And
with  the  latest  speech  reco  software,
you  can  just  talk  back  with  100%
accuracy.  Wouldn't  you  like  that,
Billy?  Oh,  and  don't  call  me  Coach
anymore. I can be Elsie, Bubeleh.
```

Billy responded:
```
K, what do i have 2 do?
```

Luci keyed:
```
Just  lay  right  there  for  a  minute,
honey. Elsie will do all the work.
```

Luci put on her wireless Sennheiser headset with the noise canceling microphone, and hit send on the subroutine command that would let her go directly though Billy's device.

###

Billy lay there, looking at his Eden phone, when the sexiest voice he had ever heard came floating out of it: "See, Billy, isn't that better?"

"Um, wow," Billy stuttered. He was actually embarrassed, and ran his fingers through his hair and brushed the pie crumbs off of his pajamas.

"Billy, I know you're lonely," Elsie aka Luci purred. "Tell Elsie what's the matter."

"Well, I thought I was happy, but for the last few weeks I've just been sitting and eating and gaining more weight, to the point where I can hardly move, and it's getting harder to breathe, too."

"Have you been eating pie again?" Elsie surmised.

"Yeah, you guessed it."

Luci quickly improvised. *Overeating—gluttony-- a nice sin. I need some toad or snake recipe*, she thought. She quickly accessed the SIM card in Billy's phone, and looked at the restaurants he had there. *Hey, look at this*, she mused. *I didn't know NY's Le Colonial French-Vietnamese restaurant had opened a new location in California and its only 5 minutes from Billy, and they deliver too.* She logged into their online menu, and ordered using Billy's Gold MasterCard number, that was stored in the device so that he could order digital ingredients for his fake pies with a touch of his fat finger.

She spoke into her microphone, "Billy, you've got too much sugar in your system. You need an honest meal. I've ordered for you Le Colonial's Bun So Diep entrée, which is grilled lemongrass scallops, shrimp and frogs' legs served with vermicelli vegetable salad, lettuce greens, fresh herbs, toasted peanuts and ginger dressing. It will be there in 10 minutes."

Billy Wilson lived for food,

Particularly pie.
He'll overeat,
His health mistreat,

"Gee, thank you, Elsie," Billy responded.

"You sound blue, Billy. Where are your friends?" Elsie asked him.

"Well, Steven is upstairs, but he's a morning person. I guess I could have used my broom handle to get him, but I hate to disturb him. I keep it here by my bed in case of emergencies, but he usually comes down in the morning to check on me."

"Billy, you don't need anyone else anymore; you have me," crooned Elsie. "Throw that broom handle away, Billy. It's just a crutch keeping you down. THROW IT NOW!"

Startled, Billy grabbed the broom handle and threw it sideways as hard as he could. It sailed through the room, and hit poor Fritz where he lay under the couch. Fritz yelped and tore into the kitchen and crouched under the table, giving off a mournful howl. Billy shook his head to clear it. What had just happened? That last command coming out of his phone seemed to have been in a totally different voice.

"There, there Billy," soothed the voice from his phone. "See how much more energy you have now without that crutch? We're making a great team, don't you think?"

Just then, there was a knock at the door. "Delivery from Le Colonial."

"Juan, is that you?" asked Billy.

"Yes, Mr. Wilson. Should I just let myself in using the key?"

"Sure, come on in, Juan."

The lock clicked, and the delivery boy entered. He was wearing a French beret and a T-shirt that read 'Le Colonial'. As he came in, a blur shot out the door. It was Mr. Wilson's dog, and though he tried to block him, Juan wasn't fast enough with his leg. He looked around the room. It was a lot worse than the last time he had been here a few weeks ago. Then, as he looked at Mr. Wilson, he noticed that his face was all coated in red gunk with streaks running through it. He tried not to stare.

"Just put it here on the bed, Juan. Did the order include a good tip for you?"

"Yes, Mr. Wilson. Fifty percent. You were most generous. I expedited your order and ran over here as fast as I could."

"Thanks, Juan. Just put the key back in its hiding place and let yourself out."

As the door closed, that voice floated out of his phone again. "Eat, Billy."

Billy did as he was ordered. He took a bite of the shrimp. Somehow it was tasteless.

"Billy, you need to eat something else," said the voice. "Try the frogs' legs."

Billy gingerly picked up a leg and put the thigh part in his mouth. Incredible flavor filled his palate. He stuffed the whole leg in his mouth, bones and all.

"Billy, faster! EAT ANOTHER," the voice commanded.

Billy stuffed another leg in, and then another. He was in a feeding frenzy. Suddenly a bone lodged deep in his throat.

He started wheezing. He couldn't get enough breath to cough.

"Billy, are you still eating?" asked the voice.

Billy wheezed a reply, "Help, Elsie. Call 911."

Suddenly a digital voice said, "Unable to recognize command. Please repeat."

"911. 911. Please…help," said Billy faintly.

"Unable to recognize command. Please repeat."

Billy fumbled for his Coach device, and manually punched in 911. The numbers were fading, but he managed.

Beep-beep-beep. Damn, trunk line busy. He tried again with the same busy signal result.

He reached for his broom handle, and then suddenly realized it was across the room under the couch. He struggled to rise, but couldn't. As night descended over his eyes, he heard his device for the last time, "Billy, don't worry, honey. You're with me now."

Billy Wilson lived for food,
Particularly pie.
He'll overeat,
His health mistreat,
Then tortuously die.

Luci typed in the command to restore Billy's SIM card to the 2.0 software. She then issued the command to delete Billy's profile from the Coach database. She removed her headset and put it back in the drawer and logged out. Then she lit a cigarette, took a puff, and blew the smoke out with a contented sigh.

13 YOU'RE FIRED!

Sam had serious concerns about Luci. Why could he find virtually nothing about her on the Internet? Where did she go to college? Where did she acquire all of her knowledge about artificial intelligence? What happened in South Korea? Was she being sought by the police? He sent Luci a text message: "Hi, Luci. Starting your press release and letter to the other investors. Please see me early AM. Bring Bio. Thanks, Sam."

Sam left for ECS Headquarters, unsure of what the day would bring. His chauffer dropped him off, wishing him a good day - he certainly needed one. The optimism and laughter of ECS in the early days was replaced now by a sense of foreboding. Today's Sunnyvale weather even reflected his mood, the corporate mood. Was it all bad luck? Was everyone overly optimistic in the early days? Was Luci just the vessel distributing bad karma?

He went into his office, gave a hesitant smile to Phyllis Johnson and walked up to his desk. Luci was already there, sitting in one of the guest chairs with her legs crossed and a cheery smile. "Good morning Sam," she started.

"Good morning, Luci. Looks like a storm today; welcome to California winters. Thanks for coming in early. This should not take long." He buzzed Phyllis. "Phyllis would you bring two black coffees, please?"

"You take your coffee black, right Luci?" Sam did not wait for an answer." OK, let's get going, I'm sure you have a busy day ahead of you. May we start with your early history? Where did you go to school?"

"I was brought up in Ireland, the daughter of two psychiatrists; my parents actually home schooled me. I wanted to go to college in the United States and was accepted at the University of Kentucky, where I majored in Mathematics and graduated Cum Laude in the year 2000. My love of math got me interested in AI and Computer Science, so I went in that direction at Kentucky doing a great deal of studying, but never obtaining a graduate degree. Instead, I started day trading and did extremely well - well enough to start some angel investments. My early investments, as I have told you, were in South Korea, my most recent one with a games developer named 'Netslate.' Have you heard of 'Netslate?'"

"I believe so," said Sam. "Please go on."

"Not much else. I made a bundle on Netslate and toyed with a few more South Korean firms. I moved to New Orleans and started my investments at Eden. The rest is recent history."

"I seem to recall something about Netslate. Wasn't there an incident that got a fair amount of press? Something about a South Korean family playing 'Nisi Online' and allowing their infant to die of starvation? Do you recall the incident, or did you leave Netslate before it happened?"

Without blinking an eyelash, Luci snapped back. "Nope. I don't recall the incident. I must have left Netslate before the unfortunate event. What a shame."

Sam now knew that he'd caught Luci in at least one lie. He'd need to do some more digging... "Thanks, Luci. If possible, would you get your college transcripts from the University of Kentucky? We should also get your Social Security Number."

This was worse than I thought, mused Sam. *Where will this end? Who in the world is this woman and what is she up to?*

"You bet. I should have everything in a few days. See you later, Sam."

Luci got up slowly from her chair and headed for the door. She thought to herself: *Sam knew too much about Netslate. He must have been doing some research. I wonder what else he knows or will find out. The University of Kentucky was a good story - their administration building burned down in 2001. I'll simply explain that they must have lost my records. A far as the Social Security Number is concerned, I'll get one forged. Meanwhile, I think it's time for Sam to leave the scene. Should be fun doing this...*

She noticed a shiny silver fountain pen on Sam's desk and surreptitiously slipped it in her purse... *I think I can put this to good use,* she chuckled to herself.

Sam sat in his office thinking after Luci had gone. *This is not going to work. We need to start curbing Luci until I can find out enough to get rid of her,* he thought. *I had better get a note to Diane; I know she shares my concerns. I'll just write her a note and slip it under her door.*

Sam looked around for his Cross® Century II Sterling Silver Fountain Pen. It had been a splurge buying the 18-carat gold nib and rhodium-plated implement, but what was the good of being a CEO if you didn't indulge in life's little pleasures now and then? "Where the hell did I leave that pen?" he muttered. Oh well, he would find it soon. He was constantly misplacing his pens, so he kept extra ones in his drawer. He grabbed a generic Paper Mate pen and a sheet of paper from his printer and wrote:

"Diane. Luci is not what she seems. Her ideas for Coach will have dire consequences. See me in the morning when you get this."

Sam sealed it in an envelope and wrote on the face "Diane, ASAP, from Sam." He then got up and walked over to Diane's office and slid the envelope under her door. Sam then got his coat, turned out the office lights, and walked out to his car.

It sure will be nice to get back to my little Hacienda Hideaway, thought Sam as he drove down the highway. *Maybe I'll sit out in my courtyard overlooking the mountains and have some Sangria. I need to relax a bit after this confrontation with Luci and think about what Diane and I can do next.*

As Sam approached his home, he noticed that the setting sun was highlighting some very large black thunderclouds that were building up near his neighborhood. *Hmm, maybe I'll sit in the covered patio instead of the courtyard. It looks like a storm is brewing. Or maybe I'll go sit in the Media Room and finally get a chance to watch that movie* The Social Network *about Facebook. Zuckerberg probably had to deal with all sorts of similar issues too, and it might give me some ideas.*

Luci pulled into the circular driveway of her brand new mission-style home, turned the car off and stared ahead. *Sam has now become a major thorn in my side with all of his snooping,* she thought. *He couldn't leave well enough alone, could he?*

Luci was also irate that Sam had discovered anything. She thought that she had covered her trail completely. Now she was going to have to do something. *Well, he's going to have to pay for that!* She slammed the car door and stomped her way to the arcaded entry porch before her front door and let herself in.

She passed through the entryway, into the foyer and turned left for the master bedroom. In her two walk-in closets were all the materials that she would need. *Let's see. Candles, check. Black hood and robe, check. Chalk, check,* she recited as she gathered them into a carryall.

As she strode back to the foyer, she tried to calm herself. This was going to take a lot out of her and she needed to be calm in order to perform the ritual correctly. If she didn't do this right, this body of hers could get torn to shreds. She didn't want to think about that. Plus it would put a serious dent in her plans.

When she reached the foyer, she sat down in front of a floor compass rosette that she had specially designed and had built into her floor. She was especially pleased with her prescience. *I'm glad I thought of this ahead of time. I sure don't want to be fussing around with compasses and twine to build a five pointed star pentagram.*

She laughed as she thought about those ancient Pythagoreans who thought they were so smart, playing around with using string and sticks to make circles and discover the secrets of geometry. Did Pythagoras really think that he had discovered all by himself the secret of the pentagon and pentagram? When it came to him in a dream that, if you connected the opposite vertices of a pentagon, you would have created a pentagram inscribed inside the pentagon, he was thrilled. And, when he saw that in the center of that created pentagram was another pentagon, inside of which you could draw another pentagram ad infinitum, he was ecstatic. The Pythagoreans even used it as a secret symbol of their brotherhood: pentagon inside pentagram inside pentagon, creating pendants that hung around their necks, which they kept hidden under their clothing. They found that after they started wearing these, they discovered even greater secrets and started worshipping the symbol. Things might have progressed from there if those Roman brutes hadn't conquered Greece and destroyed that knowledge!

"Bah, never mind that! I need to focus," she muttered. Her specially designed floor compass rose had ten points instead of the usual eight so that she could use half of them to create a perfectly symmetrical five-pointed star. She needed to make sure that she created her pentagram with two points facing up, like the horns of a goat. She slowly traced the star with the chalk, and then traced the first circle around and just touching the star. Then she carefully traced the larger circle around the whole thing.

She placed a candle at each point of the star, lit each and then turned off all of the lights. She sat herself down at the bottom point of the star and started to chant:

"Mammon, Mammon, come to me.
From the chains of hell, thou must break free.
Mammon, Mammon, I summon thee,
To slay the victim who's full of greed."

Black smoke swirled within the pentagram. Slowly it coalesced into a dark figure. Bat wings, horns, fangs, claws. Then he stood there in the pentagram, eight feet tall on two human-like legs, leering with saliva dripping from two very large fangs.

"Ah, freedom to slay! It has been a long time," Mammon boomed. "Dost thou have a village, a town, perhaps a city for me?" His forked tongue flicked out and licked his lips.

"Mammon, heed me well. There is a human here who can thwart our plans. He needs to be eliminated," said Luci with the bravest voice she could muster. If Mammon got loose without agreeing to her behest, she would have a hard time controlling him.

"WHAT? ONE HUMAN? DOST THOU SUMMON ME FOR ONLY THIS?" shouted Mammon. "Thy problems are not mine. Where are the souls I have been promised?"

"Soon, Mammon. Soon wilst thou have thousands, nay millions, to do with as thee please. This one needs to come first," Luci stated as calmly as she could. "Every journey begins with a single step. This one is that first step. Then come the rich rewards. More than a town or city or even country. A world full of victims."

That seemed to soothe Mammon. "Very well; I have waited for millennia. Perhaps a few more moments will matter not. Who is this victim?"

"His name is Sam Washburn, and he is CEO of Eden Coaching Systems. He is full of pride and greed. He wants everything for himself," she lied. "He lives lavishly and foolishly, and is meddling in our affairs. I have placed at your feet a writing implement of his, which will help you locate him. You must consume him in the time-honored way, but using a method where we do not come under suspicion. It should look like an accident."

"Mayest I take my time with him?" grinned Mammon.

"Absolutely. Begone!" commanded Luci.

With a bang and a swirl of wind, Mammon disappeared, and Luci lay back exhausted. She had taken a big chance summoning Mammon, since Sam was no greedier than any other human. Still, he needed to be eliminated along with many others. To paraphrase that old Abbot and Papal Legate, when asked who deserved to be killed after a medieval city was captured, "Kill them all, and let God sort them out!" *Sam, you're about to be added to the list of those being sorted*, she chuckled silently.

As Sam pulled into his driveway and pressed the remote to open the garage door, a deluge started pouring down from the sky. *Damn, first time the weathermen have gotten a forecast right in weeks! Just my luck,* he thought.

He got out of his car and went through the door into his house, and passed through the 19-foot vaulted Great Room with its entry tower and into the kitchen. He dumped his keys, wallet and Eden smartphone on the island, and pulled a bottle of wine out of the fridge, poured himself a drink and walked through the house to the covered patio. The wind was really whipping outside, so he turned on the custom-made fire pit that ran off of the house's oil tank. As he looked out through the screens, he thought he saw a dark shape flit amongst the trees. *How weird*, he thought. *It's probably just a reflection from the flames, but I never noticed it before.*

As Sam sat on the couch sipping his wine and staring at the fire, he thought about what he and Diane should do tomorrow. *Perhaps we should get the police involved,* he thought. *Luci seems to have been dealing in some nefarious activities in the past, but we don't have any real evidence yet. We'll have to get some. Maybe she's been doing something like tampering with our email system. We just need to find one reason.*

Sam pulled out the small pad that he always kept handy in his jacket pocket, fumbled out the Paper Mate pen and wrote, "Ask Diane to review Luci's access logs, " thought about it some more, and then wrote, "Call police to investigate Luci."

Whoosh.

Suddenly, the flame pit flared about eight feet high. Sam tried pushing back with his feet, but the couch was bolted into the floor. He quickly reached forward to push the button to extinguish the flame, but nothing happened. He whipped off his jacket and tried smothering the flame, but all he succeeded in doing was setting his jacket on fire and singeing the hairs on his arms.

Oh great, now I have black oil smoke in here too! Adrenalin pumping, he reached forward and tried the shut-off button again, and this time the flames shrank and then went out with a pop.

He fanned the horribly stinky smoke away from his face. Suddenly, the wind howled outside and blew the smoke into one corner of the room, where it swirled briefly, and then at that moment the lights flickered and went out.

As the wind howled, Sam saw a hideous face in the corner where the smoke was. The few remaining hairs on his arms stood on end, and then the automatic generator kicked in and the lights returned.

There was nothing in the corner.

Luci got up from the floor. *Stupid, stupid, stupid*, she grumbled. *I forgot to disable Sam's Coach.*

She hurried over to one of the spare bedrooms that she had set up as a home office, and logged into Eden's systems. All employees were issued home IDs for login at any time of the day or night that they wished to work, and Coach smartphones for personal use as a matter of policy.

She looked up Sam's phone ID in the system. *No time to download anything fancy to his phone,* she thought. *I'll just invoke the stolen device routine for his device to disable all functions. Then later I'll just reverse it, and no one will be the wiser.* It was just a matter of moments for the command to take effect.

Luci leaned back and took a deep breath. That was too close. She couldn't afford any mistakes right now.

As she logged off, she didn't realize that the remote login system had created a record of her having accessed the Eden security system.

Sam looked again. Nope, there was still nothing in that corner. *I've been watching too many horror movies*, he mused. *After watching* The Ring *last month, I was creeped out each time I went to the bathroom in the middle of the night, thinking I would see that awful girl. I'm glad that stopped after a week.*

Sam noticed his note pad sitting on the floor next to the pen. He picked it up and wrote, "Call maintenance to fix fire pit," and put the notepad in his back pocket.

Sam walked back through the kitchen to the Great Room, heading towards the Tool room. He needed to get a wrench to turn off the oil shut-off valve to the fire pit until he could call and arrange for the repair guys. As he walked, the whole house shook.

Knock, knock, knock

Sam stopped. No one would be out here in this storm, would they? He walked over and opened the front door. Nobody. The wind was really howling now and it was almost pitch black. *Geez, this could be a tropical storm the way it is out here,* he thought. As he started to close the door, he thought he saw that hideous face from the corner above the bushes. He leaned further out and squinted.

Whoosh, snap

Sam felt a searing pain in his left hand and looked down. A twig was sticking out of the back of his hand! He slammed the door shut with his right hand, and hustled back towards the kitchen. There was a bathroom near there to get some bandages. As he ran, he looked more closely at his aching left hand. The object was sticking out both ends of his hand! It had gone right through!

Wait, is that my silver Cross pen? How the hell did that get here? He grabbed the pen and flung it away with a grimace. Blood started flowing freely from the wound. He didn't notice that the black cloud had reappeared and directed the pen towards his fire pit, puncturing the tube that fed oil to the device.

As he reached the kitchen, all the drawers flew open and utensils started flying at him. He ducked.

"Fuck this shit," he yelled. "I'm outta here!" He reached for his Eden phone, which was sitting, right there on the counter, and ran back towards the entryway. He swiped his finger across the face of the device.

DISABLED popped up on the screen.

"WHAT?" screamed Sam. He tried it again with the same result.

Suddenly, there was a roar behind him. He glanced back, and saw a horrid apparition. It looked like a huge demon reaching for him.

Sam yelped and backpedaled to retreat, when suddenly his left foot slipped on oil that had leaked and spread all over the floor. He fell, getting disgusting oil all over himself. As he started to rise, his front door swung wide and a blast of wind pushed him stumbling backwards towards his porch, his feet pinwheeling over the oil.

Unluckily for Sam, his flailing body landed right on the fire pit, which flared suddenly to life, causing a huge fireball when it ignited the oil coating him. The last thing he saw was that hideous demonic being dancing in the flames.

CEO Washburn made his plans;
He'd stretch out by the fire.
He failed to see
The real Luci -
Would cause his funeral pyre.

14 NOT BY BREAD ALONE

"And so, in Mathew 4:1-11, we see that Satan is called 'the Tempter' and rightly so. Jesus was also a man, and thus subject to our same foibles and weaknesses. In the first temptation, Satan said to Jesus, 'If you are the Son of God, command these stones to become loaves of bread.' Jesus answered, "Man shall not live by bread alone…"'

Brinnggg, brinnggg.

Father Murphy stopped, and all heads in the church turned.

"Ant'ney! I told you not to leave that phone turned on during Mass!" Marie hissed.

Marone, it was going to be another one of those days, thought Detective Anthony "Tony" Magnini as he peeked at his cell phone. He couldn't believe the precinct was calling him at 7:50 am on a Sunday. This had better be a doozie. He hauled his 6'2" 230 pound frame up, moved left, genuflected, crossed himself and walked down the center aisle to the back of the church. As he did so, every head turned back to Father Murphy as he droned on.

Tony answered the call, "Magnini."

"Tony, I'm glad you picked up. I've been trying your damned partner for 15 minutes and he won't answer! We got a 911 from over in Lafayette Park on an apparent homicide of some fat guy and I need you to go investigate," explained Police Captain John Macfee. "Some witness was apparently screaming hysterically about all the blood to the 911 operator. Get that partner of yours and haul your asses over there. Here's the address."

Tony took down the information on a pad he always kept with him, and then brought up his cell phone contact list. His captain didn't know that Tony's partner kept a separate private number for situations just like this. There it was, first in the list for easy dialing: AA-James Tyler Kirkland. He pressed the number.

"Lo," came a muffled answer on the fifth ring.

"Jim, get UP. The Cap's been trying to reach you."

"Wha' time is it?" mumbled Jim.

"It's almost 8am. This is what you get for not going to church on a Sunday. Were you up all night carousing again?"

"Yeah, I wish!" said Jim, slowly coming awake. "Ever since Suzie moved out, I've ended up watching late night TV and playing video games since I just can't get to sleep. Why are you calling so early?"

"I told you, the Cap's been trying to reach you, and he's really P.O.'ed you didn't answer. It looks like there's been a homicide near Lafayette Park, and we need to get over there ASAP," said Tony. "Get dressed, I'll be right over."

Tony debated going back to let his wife know what was going on, but hated having to walk all the way to the front where she liked to sit while everyone stared at him. *Oh, hell, she'll figure it out,* he thought. *Marie has lots of friends here at church; she can catch a ride with one of them.*

Tony went over to his unmarked squad car that he always used, pulled into traffic and then hopped on the MacArthur Freeway. Soon he was at Jim's place. Jim was waiting outside. *God, to be 29 again,* thought Tony as he looked at his partner. *No sleep and he looks rarin' to go. I guess it helps having a blond crew cut,* he thought as he glanced at his 55-year-old face and his salt and pepper hair in the rear view mirror.

"What are you starin' at, old man?" asked Jim, as he

slipped into the passenger seat. "Put this puppy in gear and let's move! Where we going?"

"We got an apparent homicide in a second floor apartment near Lafayette," said Tony. "It seems that the neighbor was quite hysterical when he called 911."

Since traffic was fairly light, Tony was happy that they were there in about 15 minutes. He double-parked the car in front of the address the captain had given him, got out of the car, and he and his partner walked up to the second floor.

It was pure chaos inside the apartment. It looked like a hoarder lived here; there were dishes of half-eaten food all over the place. On a bed in one corner was this huge guy with people milling all around him taking pictures.

"This is a crime scene! Get out now!" bellowed Tony, sending two people scrambling for the exit to the apartment. "Who's responsible for securing this place?"

Rob, the coroner, came over. "Um, sorry Tony. We were pretty much waiting for you guys to arrive. It's not a homicide, so we weren't worried too much about tampering."

Tony looked at the guy lying on the bed. There were plates all over him and the bed covers. It looked like there was blood all over his face and neck. "So, Rob, what's all that stuff on his face? The information we had said that the guy who called it in said there was tons of blood."

"Oh, that's actually cherry pie filling," Rob said. "It looks like he had dinner last night of frogs' legs, and cherry pie for dessert. You can't believe some of the stuff I've seen in peoples' guts when dissecting..."

"Uh, enough, Rob," said Jim. "Not this early in the day, please!"

"So what was the cause of death?" asked Tony.

"Well, it looks like it was slow suffocation. This guy must weigh all of 500 pounds. It probably took hours for him to die, and it was most likely pretty agonizing."

"Why didn't he call 911 if it took so long?" asked Jim.

"That's a good question," said Rob. "There's one of those fancy cell phone/tablet gadgets on his bed next to him."

"OK, make sure no one touches it," said Tony. "Where's the guy who called it in. We need to talk to him."

"He's in the other room. His name is Steven Schulman, and he lives upstairs. It seems he came down to check on the deceased early this morning, and let himself in when there was no answer. That's all I know."

Tony led the way into the next room. At a kitchen table, a sixty something year old mousy looking fellow was sitting with his head in his hands. Tony walked over to him.

"Excuse me, are you Mr. Schulman? I'm Detective Magnini, and this is Detective Kirkland. Can you come outside with us where it is a little quieter? We just need to ask you a few questions."

Mr. Schulman nodded, got up, and walked out the apartment door onto the hallway landing.

"Mr. Schulman, what do you know about the deceased?" asked Jim.

"Poor Billy! His name is Billy Wilson you know. Wouldn't hurt a fly. I can't believe this has happened!"

"How did you discover him?"

"Well, I always check on Billy. He has a very hard time getting out and about, due to his size. We've been friends for years. I live right above him. If he needs anything, he takes a broom handle and bangs three times on the ceiling. We got the idea from that old Tony Orlando and Dawn song, you know."

Jim looked quizzically at Mr. Schulman. "Before your time," said Tony. He then added, "The coroner said that this took quite some time. Why didn't he signal you, do you think?"

"I don't know! I didn't see his broom handle anywhere when I came in. Maybe the killer beat him with it and then took it?" Mr. Schulman asked.

Tony realized that no one had told Mr. Schulman that it wasn't blood on the body, so he explained that Mr. Wilson had died from suffocation.

"How did you get in here, Mr. Schulman?" asked Jim. "Do you have a key?"

"Yes, but I misplace it constantly. Billy leaves one stuck here on the door so that delivery boys can leave him his groceries and food deliveries. It's inside this hollow mezuzah taped on the doorpost. Billy was good with his hands, you know."

Now it was Tony who was stumped. "Mezuzah?"

"Oh, it's this little thing here. It's put on the right side of doors in Jewish households and holds a piece of parchment with words on it in Hebrew. Billy opened it up and put the key inside. I told him that he was invalidating the Torah by removing the parchment, but he wasn't Jewish and said that he didn't care. He told me it was better than hiding the key in fake poop or under the doormat. He told me that he learned about mezuzahs from a college roommate. I told him that the words on the parchment have 'the Lord our God' in Hebrew and helps to protect a household and that he shouldn't do it, but he just wouldn't listen!" Mr. Schulman moaned.

"OK, thanks, Mr. Schulman," Tony stated. "You should go back upstairs and rest. We'll come up if we have any additional questions."

Tony and Jim walked back inside the apartment. It looked like things were wrapping up.

"Rob, how are you going to get this huge guy out of here?" asked Jim.

"They're calling in a cherry picker to take him out the window. No way we're taking him down a flight of stairs. I'm not even sure we could get him out the door!"

"Well, good luck with that!" said Tony. He walked over to the bed, put on gloves, and picked up the cell phone/tablet. He handed it to Jim, who had also put gloves on. "Here, Jim. You're good with these newfangled gadgets. What's on it?"

Jim slid his finger across the screen and tapped a few times on the smartphone. "Hmm, it looks like it's full of phone numbers for bakeries, fast food places, and restaurants that deliver. Let me check what apps are on it."

"What are apps?" asked Tony.

"Geez, Tony, don't your grandkids have smartphones and tablets when they come to visit you and Marie? Apps are computer applications that run on those devices. They can do all sorts of amazing things. Let me see…yup. He's got a bunch. Man, this guy was addicted to this stuff. Look here at the icons: 'Pie Creator', 'Restaurant Story', 'Bakery Time'. What a list!"

"What do they do?" asked Tony.

"These are games that let you do things like create your own pies and share them with others who have the application. Or you can run a bakery. Little computer people come and sit down and you serve them, and then they get up and pay. The more they pay you, the more game money you have to buy more seats, ovens and ingredients. The app companies make money because people become impatient and pay real money to buy the game money instead of playing for days to earn enough to purchase the fancy goodies."

Tony shook his head. "With all this stuff he could do, why didn't he call 911 or any friends?"

"That's a good question. Let's see what the lab guys can get off the SIM card when we bring it back," said Jim.

Tony and Jim headed for the door. As they went out, Tony took one look back. The guys were opening the window. *Huh*, thought Tony. *A cherry picker. I bet the guy never saw that coming when he was eating that cherry pie for the last time.*

15 SERPENT SAGA

The San Francisco Chronicle: "… Police have begun an investigation into the mysterious death of Samuel J. Washburn, CEO of Eden Coaching Systems (ECS). The badly charred remains of Mr. Washburn, 49, were found along side of the fire pit in the rear of his Pacific Heights home. While the initial assumptions made by the local police were that this was a freak accident, authorities from the central San Francisco area are being called in to assist in the investigation of this high-profile death. Sergeant Kevin Collins of the San Francisco Northern Station was quoted as saying: 'We were called in by the Pacific Heights Fire Department after they responded to a report of a fire at Mr. Washburn's estate. While we are fairly certain that Mr. Washburn died as the result of an unfortunate accident in yesterday's storm, we are treating his death as a potential homicide and securing his home as a crime scene. There will be further announcements…'

Mr. Washburn was regarded as a visionary within the electronics community. He was the brainchild behind the ECS Coach, a smartphone with an artificial intelligence underpinning....

... Mr. Washburn apparently had no surviving relatives, except for his estranged wife Joan, a resident of Los Angeles...."

The ECS Executive Board sat once again around the conference table, the day after Sam's funeral. Luci was dressed in a simple black dress, holding a handkerchief in her right hand. She sat in Sam's slot at the head of the glass table. Ian sat to her right, staring perplexedly into space. Rose, also seemingly bewildered, sat at Luci's left. Joe and Diane were seated together at the far end of the table; both of them had obviously been crying. Luci started the meeting.

"Like the rest of you, I was stunned and saddened by Sam's death. I'm personally thankful for his helping me to get on board and integrated with the Eden team. Maybe we can start with a moment of silence?"

"Better yet," spoke Diane from the rear of the room, "may I say a short prayer?"

"I'd prefer that we do so silently," said Luci. "Not all of us worship God."

After a brief pause, Luci continued. "We need to start now to pick up the pieces and move on. After all, it is what Sam would wish of us.

Let me first say that I have engaged an executive search firm to start looking for Sam's replacement. The search process will take a fair amount of time so, during the interim period, I shall serve as the Eden CEO. It's entirely possible that one of you is qualified to be CEO, so I'm not excluding that possibility. I'll just need to get to know each of you better in the next few months.

As you all know, Sam had a large number of Eden shares. As an incentive to you, I'll start the legal proceedings to distribute his shares evenly among you. May I count on your help, Joe?"

Joe wiped his eyes. "I'd be glad to help you with this task, Luci. Some of you know that I joined ECS solely because I was a very good friend of Sam's. Sam is gone, so my preference is to leave ECS after I've helped Luci with a few loose ends. Luci, would you kindly have the executive search firm look for my replacement?"

Luci tried her best to conceal a smirk. "Sure, Joe. Thank you for all your efforts thus far. I'll set up a meeting with you to review your remaining tasks. Is anyone else having thoughts about leaving? I would hope not, as I plan to make good on my promise to make all of you wealthy."

Diane had read Sam's note about Luci "not being what she seems." She was now absolutely sure that something was up with Luci, but what? Sam's death was an accident, or was it? She did not trust Luci one bit but she'd play it safe and keep quiet. She'd need some help in getting to the bottom of her nagging concerns, but to whom should she turn? She could trust Joe but was unsure about the others. She'd start by meeting with a friend and confidant, Ted Johnson her pastor.

Luci continued... "I'd like to meet with each of you privately to go over any concerns you may have and I'll set up those meetings starting tomorrow.

Release 3.0 will be coming soon, so I'd like to start a major push. I'm asking that we leave Sunday mornings open for staff meetings so that we can focus our time effectively during the normal workweek. I know that some of you have family obligations, but the Sunday commitment will just be for the short time prior to the 3.0 release."

Diane cringed. Sunday was the most important day of the week for her. Church and then family. This woman was something else... Luci saw the expression on Diane's face. "Don't worry about the press release, Diane. I'll write the press release about my taking over on an interim basis. You'll help me distribute it through your connections."

Luci brushed her right leg against Ian's. "Ian, would you mind staying late tonight? I need to go over the development schedule with you, item by item..."

"Press Release: For Immediate Distribution

Sunnyvale, California

ECS Announces Interim Organization

Luci Ferguson, acting CEO of Eden Coaching Systems, provided the following details about ECS organizational changes: 'After the tragic death of our CEO, Samuel Washburn, we have the following organizational announcements: Firstly, I shall act as interim CEO until we conclude our search for a qualified replacement. Secondly, I have reluctantly accepted the resignation of Joseph Bernstein, Legal Counsel. We are actively pursuing a search for his replacement. Lastly, our other divisional executives remain in place and are committed to making our next major release, Coach 3.0, a groundbreaking success. Our Vice President of Marketing, Diane Jones, will make details about the features and functions of the Coach 3.0 release available in the following weeks.'

Luci Ferguson is the majority stockholder of ECS. She has an extensive background in both gaming systems and artificial intelligence, and a Bachelor Of Science from the University of Kentucky."

16 AT PLAY IN THE GARDEN

Luci had set up her one-on-ones with the ECS vice presidents. Her first scheduled meeting was another evening rendezvous with Ian. Luci sauntered into Ian's office and closed his door. She then slowly removed all but her bra and panties. "Ready for playtime?" she asked.

Ian laughed. "You never get enough, do you? My job has amazing residual benefits.

How did you survive the day, Luci? Sam was a good guy, you know. I'll miss him. We all will miss him. He treated us well."

"And I'll treat you just as well. You know that, right? You and I are joined at the hip. We'll be good partners and carry on famously, despite Sam's loss."

"I have no reason to believe otherwise." Ian smiled. "Do we have any business to discuss?"

"Just one. One of our users sent Eden a nice note. Seems he has identified a number of 'friends' in his social media searches. He knows where they live and a little bit about them, but he wants to find their whereabouts in real-time. We have the data kicking around from the social media feeds, correct? Could we make his request a 4.0 requirement?"

"Maybe, Luci. If someone says they're in a mall or movie theater and they click on one of our icons, then that person becomes 'a live target' for others to locate. If, then, you wanted to find your friend 'Joe Schmoe' you could type in his name in a 'location search' and either we'd say 'location unavailable' or we'd specify his location. Would that be OK?"

"Sounds good. Let me talk to this guy. His name is Eric

Kruger.

Ready for the real business?"

The next morning, Luci had an 8:00 with Diane Jones. Diane was tense. She had trouble sleeping the night before. *What did Sam mean in his note about Luci not being what she appeared to be? Should I ask questions about Luci's background or just shut up and listen? I've always had bad vibes... I think I'll just be polite and let her ask questions. I don't want to say too much...*

"Good Morning, Diane." Luci started the dialogue. "Glad we could sit and talk for a while. Coffee?"

"No thank you, Luci. I'm just fine."

"OK, then. Tell me about yourself. I've read your *curriculum vitae*. You have an impressive background. But tell me about your personal life."

"Not very exciting. I've been married for about four years and we have one two-year old boy. My husband Charlie and I value our time together. Family life is very important. We have little or no time for sports or hobbies. Boring life, I guess."

Luci smirked. "You grimaced a bit when I called our staff meetings for Sunday mornings. I take it you are religious?"

How do I answer this one? Diane thought quickly. "I guess so. We go to church every Sunday. I teach Sunday school. You said you do not believe in God. Are you an atheist?"

Luci gave her standard answer. She'd never tell anyone the truth, as no one would believe it. "No, Diane. I'm actually a very spiritual person. All souls are connected. We are all part of nature. That kind of spiritual. I just don't believe in a personal God. I hope our differences won't cause us any strife." *Yep. People who don't believe in God say this all the time. If they only knew the truth.*

"Of course not, Luci. You are entitled to your beliefs and your opinions."

"Wonderful. I have one more topic. The marketing slogan for 3.0. I've suggested 'What's your pleasure?' to be consistent with much of the Coach 3.0 interactive dialogue. I know you have trouble with that, but I'll make you an offer. If the slogan and 3.0 are not a huge success, I'll let you choose any slogan you want. Deal?"

What is this woman up to? Can I trust anything she says? "I guess."

"Very well then. Oh, by the way. I have a good idea for a visual to go with the slogan. May I show it to you?"

"Sure! Let's see it."

Luci brought out a large photograph of herself reclining on a sofa, scantily clad and holding a half-empty martini glass. The caption read: "What's your pleasure?"

"How do you like it, Diane? Sex sells, you know. In fact, I think we should put it on the box cover too."

Diane turned several shades of red and dismissed herself from the room. She could not wait to meet with her pastor.

Rose Chen sat nervously in her office looking at her desk clock. She wasn't sure what these one-on-ones with Luci were all about. Was Luci looking to cut staff and bring in her own people now that Sam was gone, in spite of her assurances to the contrary? Was Luci looking for an excuse to lay her off? Rose really needed this job, and she was good at it and worked her butt off. She would make sure that Luci knew during the meeting that she would do anything for the company.

At 1:00 pm sharp she walked over to Luci's office and knocked on the open door. "Hi, Luci, are you ready for me?"

"Yes, come right in, Rose," said Luci. "You might be worried about the reason for this meeting, so let's get that out of the way first. I'm not looking to fire anybody right now. I'll be honest with you -- I've done things like that in the past, but no one currently here deserves that.

As long as you are ready to do what it takes to make Eden a success, then we'll get along just fine. What I really wanted to do is to get to know what makes my employees tick, so that I can get the most out of them while making their dreams come true. Tell me how you ended up here."

"Well, there's really not much to tell. I was the first one in my family to go to college, and luckily it was on a scholarship since my family could not afford to send me. I received my degree in Economics. I was always interested in money, since we didn't have any when I was growing up."

"Your family must be very proud of you," said Luci.

"Sometimes I wonder. They came over from China when I was very little and opened a Chinatown restaurant. We lived above it with my grandparents and my aunts and uncles all crammed into three rooms. I was their only child, and they never failed to remind me that I had to do well since many baby girls in China are killed. It's a consequence of the one-child policy there; parents want their one child to be a male so that he can provide for them in their old age. My parents are still there, running that restaurant, and I send them a little money every month."

"So what did you do before you came here?"

"I started at MySpace in its heyday, right when they wanted to monetize it, but I was too late for the stock options. It wouldn't have mattered anyway since they went down the tubes pretty quickly." Rose shook her head. "They wouldn't listen to me. The quality of the site went downhill pretty fast since they bombarded users with highly irrelevant ads, many of them of a sexual nature. The whole site became unusable as they lost control to the advertisers.

After that, I drifted into other jobs but I was never early enough for them to really pay off. Then, my parents tried to marry me off to a Chinese fellow named Huang Li, who used to come into their restaurant. They kept going on about how smart he was and how he could help take care of me and the whole family, but it didn't work out. There was no way I was going to marry someone I hardly knew and sit around the house all day eating potato chips and watching soap operas. He was also more interested in some weird hobbies he had, and, well, this is going to sound like a really strange coincidence."

"Go on," said Luci intrigued.

"Huang had been Ian McIntyre's roommate at Stanford. I met Ian at a New Year's party that he held, and he couldn't stop talking about how this new startup he had joined was so much better than any other company out there. When he found out that I had worked at MySpace and at similar startups, he got all excited and hooked me up with an interview, and, well, here I am."

"So what do you plan on doing when we're successful?"

"I'd like to retire and live in Barbados. Some of my girlfriends and I went there many years ago during a summer vacation. None of us had any money, but we managed to get a really cheap apartment for a week that used to house some U.S. military personnel. It was off the main street, and had no hot water, but I still loved it. The beaches were all behind these really expensive hotels, but the beaches were public and so you could just walk around the hotel and swim and sunbathe all day.

At night, we would go to the nearby hotel and just order a drink, and we would get to watch whatever show was being put on that night for free! Sometimes it would be fire dancers or fire-eaters. I still remember the 'Limbo Queen' who could get underneath a bar that was about two feet high. Then we would go out and walk along the beach and watch the little crabs run in and out of the surf. It was just gorgeous."

"You make it sound lovely."

"Well, sometimes it wasn't. There was a bull tied up next to the apartment that would bellow loudly all night long since he wanted to get to the cows, so we hardly got any sleep.

And you took your hearing and your life in your hands if you decided to forgo the blue government bus for transportation and instead took the faster yellow bus. The yellow buses were privately run, and had Rasta guys that sped and took all sorts of chances passing on the one lane roads, all while blaring Reggae music at ear splitting levels. I even found a K-tel tape in the store of yellow bus music that I sometimes play when I'm blue. I smile as I think of the small children in their school uniforms hanging on for dear life as the bus caromed around. I'm pretty sure that the 'Night Bus' in the Harry Potter movie was based on them," Rose said with a dreamy smile.

"So that's where you want to go?"

"Yes, but this time I want to live in the rich section of the island where there are no bulls and go to the hotels and afford real dinners of flying fish and let them come serve me drinks on the beach. And I want a convertible where I can wave at the yellow buses as they pass me by. And I want to be able to afford to go scuba diving and take the submarine tour of the ocean floor."

"But what about your family?" Luci asked.

"Oh yeah, you're right; they would never move there. I would buy them a nice house and give them money to visit China again. They would like that."

"Rose, stick with me and you'll have all of that and more. I hear that horse racing is big there. How about owning a racehorse and having your own box at the track? I bet you would like that too," Luci said.

"Wow, that really would be great! Do you really think that's possible? I would do anything for you if I could live that life."

"That's my girl; that's what I want to hear. You do exactly what I say, and you'll get everything you deserve."

Now for some fun, thought Luci. She sent Eric Kruger a text message:
```
Hi, Eric. Elsie from Eden here. Can u
talk?
```

Eric responded,
```
Sure. What's up?
```

```
I want to discuss your tracking
requirement. I'm one of the analysts
here who is working on future versions
of our systems. I'll call your Coach
phone now, OK?
```

Luci called Eric and started the conversation. "Sorry we took some time to respond to your request. You probably know that we had quite a tragedy here."

"Yes. I read about it. Mr. Washburn was quite an innovator."

"Indeed he was. We all miss him greatly. But let's talk about your requirement. I understand that you want to use your Coach to track your friends. We might be able to put this kind of tracking into version 4.0 which is scheduled for release in about eight months."

"Eight months? I was hoping to connect with them earlier..."

"Let me see what I can do personally," said Luci. "Meanwhile let me tell you how it would work.

We'd have an app called something like 'find friends.' You'd enter the name of someone on your contact list and then we'd check to see if we knew that person's location. If we knew his or her location, we'd respond with that information on an interactive map. If not, we'd say 'location unavailable.' Would that work for you?"

"I guess so. How do you get the location information?"

"We would access this information through one of our social media partners. Most people don't know that veritably all smartphones transmit their GPS locations by default. We know, for example, that the smartphone ads that get the most clicks are from people sitting in movie theaters waiting for the movie to start. We also know that ads get many responses from fishermen waiting for a bite, and we know that they are fishermen since their GPS locations show them sitting still in the middle of a lake! There's even a term for this; it's called 'reality mining.'

I've got an idea though. You have my phone number, so why not text me when you want to track someone. If I have the time, I'll hook you up with the information. This would be a good test of your tracking requirement, so I don't mind helping you out."

"That would be wonderful, Elsie. Thank you very much. I'll text you in a few days."

Luci said goodbye and then danced happily around her chair. She knew of course what Eric had in mind. She knew it from his profile indicating frequent visits to child porn sites. She knew that his friends would be teenage girls. She'd be very happy to help Eric when the time came.

Eric Kruger liked his girls;
He watched them on his street.
He'll track them down,
All over town,

17 MORE TOYS FOR LUCI

Luci really enjoyed the time she was spending with ECS customers. She needed to have a few more sessions. *Billy Wilson represented gluttony, Eric Kruger lust. How about greed? That should be easy,* she thought.

She started another search of the customer base: QUERY salary>$1M

The response came back:
43 RESULTS. PRINT?

That search is not telling me enough. What else can I try? Just for a lark, let's try this...

QUERY salary>$1M AND searchword=ponzi

1 RESULT, PRINT?

Wow. Some wealthy guy was recently spending some time looking at Ponzi schemes. Atta girl, Luci, you hit the jackpot. She hit "VIEW."

Luci opened up the profile: ELIZABETH SILVER. *So Elizabeth Silver and her husband ran Silver Investments, LLC.* Luci searched the Web for "Silver Investments" and eventually found the business' website. *Looks like they are doing well for themselves, so why should they be looking at Ponzi schemes? Gotta check this out...*

Elizabeth will suspect something if I just call her up. I can't play "analyst" as I did with Eric. What if I pose as the new "voice of Coach?" Luci tried the same trick she had done with Billy, but with a new twist that Ian had shown her. The development team had installed a software backdoor for remote debugging of users' devices. When Elizabeth Silver would next initiate a verbal request on her Coach, she would instead call Luci. Luci would field her request, but in this case she would imitate the standard Coach woman's voice, and jump into Lizzy's life.

The next morning, Lizzy Silver picked up here Coach. She hit the "REQUESTS" button and spoke. "Any successful Ponzi schemes?" The call went to Luci.

Luci was still half asleep, rolling around in her satin sheets. She picked up her Coach and immediately recognized Lizzy's number. She thought quickly. "Yes. A few. May I send you a list?"

"No."

"Are you looking to raise some money?"

"Yes"

Perfect, thought Luci. "Coach can help you. Sign up as an advertiser and Coach can target clients for you. You can then contact them directly. Will that help?"

"Yes"

Lizzy Silver could not believe her good fortune. She rushed in to see her husband Fred. Fred was in the kitchen gulping down his second cup of coffee.

"Hey, Fred. I think this Coach thing might help us. If we sign up as an advertiser, Coach can find new clients for us. I told you that Coach might help!"

"Hold on, Liz. We still have two unknowns. What exactly will we offer those new clients? How effectively can Coach target them?"

Liz sat down across the kitchen table from Fred. "I've been thinking about this a lot, Fred. Many of our large clients are Jewish. Madoff was successful in his appeals to his Jewish clients, so why not us? They won't suspect us because, unlike Madoff, we actually did invest their money. It was just our bad luck that our software bug made them all invest at outrageously high price levels. We just won't tell them the truth. We're well connected through our temple. We have our philanthropic connections. Suppose we were to research a set of Israeli tech startups and say that we are gathering up 'seed money.' We could put together an impressive portfolio. You and I could invite clients to our home for dinner, ply them with alcohol and give them one helluva dog and pony show. What do you think?"

Fred had to voice his concerns. "Can we really get away with this? What if they track your conversations with Coach? How do we pull it off? Where do we stash the money?"

"No problem, Fred. This is our time to leverage all of the pro-Israel sentiment. We could put the money into a Swiss account and tell the investors that we're going to travel to Israel to do all of our funding in one shot. I think it could work. As far as tracking our Coach conversations is concerned, we'll be long gone in a safe haven."

Fred finally smiled. "So we'd take the money and skip town to the Riviera instead, right?"

"Yep. Or someplace like it. The timing would be critical. Let's put our heads together and start the ball rolling. I'll research the ECS Advertising Program, OK?"

"Sounds like a plan, hon. I'll dig into our existing customer base for likely prospects. We'll need to check our list against those coming from ECS." Fred went over to his computer.

After a half hour or so, Lizzy composed herself. She picked up her Coach a second time. "Can you help with advertising?" The request, of course, bounced to Luci.

"Our Advertising Director will call you right back. May she call you at this number?"

"Yes"

After a few minutes, Luci called Liz back in her normal voice.

"Good afternoon. Elizabeth?"

"This is she, but please call me Liz. With whom am I speaking?"

Luci quickly used her pseudonym. "My name is Elsie Rodgers. How may I help you?"

"We had some detailed questions about your targeting capabilities. Can you target by religion or ethnicity?"

"No problem."

Lizzy thought a bit. "I assume you can target by salary level, but with what granularity?"

"Any clip level you like." Luci was ready to set the hook. "Tell you what. We normally charge a higher rate for complex targeting, but I'll give you the normal rates and handle this personally for you. Send the details by email to 'elsie.rodgers@edencoachingsystems.com' and I'll take care of everything for you." Luci was ecstatic. This one would really be fun because she'd drag many others into the morass.

Lizzy was dumbfounded. This was too good to be true. "Well, er thank you, Elsie. We'll be in touch in a week or so."

And so, Luci was off and running again.

Lizzy Silver loved her gold;
She watched her wealth recede.
She'd get it back

###

Detective Tony Magnini steeled himself for the storm that was to come as he opened the door to his house. "Honey, I'm home!" he called as he stepped over the threshold. He held a dozen roses in his hand that he had bought on his way back from that fat guy's murder scene.

"Ant'ney Benedetto Magnini, you've got a lot of nerve!" yelled his wife Marie from the kitchen. "This is your typical fine 'how-de-do!' after you've screwed up. You couldn't come tell me you were leaving the church? I had to beg for a ride from the Hernandez family down the block. And you've been gone for hours without even a call home!"

Tony walked into the kitchen. Marie had her back turned to him and was vigorously chopping carrots, probably for tonight's dinner. He snuck up behind her and put his arms around her, waving the flowers. "C'mon honey. Don't be mad. See? I bought you some flowers."

Marie slapped his hand and whipped around, waving the knife in his face, her brown eyes blazing at him. "Do you think some stupid flowers are gonna make up for leaving me alone at church? Who knows what everyone was thinking as I sat there all alone and, you missed Communion. You're going to hell for sure. I might send you there myself right now!" she fumed as she waved the knife in the air, turned around, and started chopping carrots again.

Tony took a deep breath and put his arms back around his wife. "C'mon honey. You know I didn't have any choice, and you knew it would be like this when we got married. Just think. Soon I'll be retired and we will have all the time in the world. We'll finally get to make that trip to Rome I promised you and see the sights." Tony kissed the back of Marie's neck and continued. "Mmmm, I love the way you smell. You're such a good cook, honey. I really don't deserve you. Whatcha makin'?"

"You don't deserve me all right, you big lug," Marie said. She couldn't help but smile. *In spite of all his faults, Tony really is a good husband and is great with the grandkids,* she thought. *I guess it's not his fault that his job keeps pulling him away. I just worry every time he goes out that something evil will happen.* "I'm making eggplant rollatini with carrots, just like you like them, even though I don't know why after what you put me through," she sighed. She turned back around to give Tony a kiss and shrieked. "What's that? Is that blood on your shirt? Oh my God, were you shot?"

"No, no. I'm fine, honey." Tony looked down at himself. "Oh, I think that's just some cherry pie filling. We had to go investigate some stiff who overate himself to death, and he had these empty pie tins all over the place. What a mess."

"You know I don't like to hear about your awful cases. Just get ready for dinner."

"Aw, honey, you're the best. I tell you what. I'll put these flowers in a jar on the table. How about some candlelight too? It'll be just the two of us."

"Don't you ever listen to me? Did you forget that Tommy and Debbie with the three grandkids are coming over tonight for Sunday dinner? They'll be here in about an hour. Go set the table and wash up! And change your shirt. We don't want the kids to think we live like animals."

18 LUCI AND THE PRINCESS

Chandra Razdan (nee Chandra Chopra) had moved to Washington DC. She and her husband Raj had purchased a luxury condominium on 14th Street. Just before they moved in, Chandra had bought her very own Coach. She was currently using her Coach to line up the help that she would need around the house: a cleaning lady and a cook, for starters. Finally, her life was beginning to align with her expectations. All she had to do was consistently "fake it" in bed with Raj and she would have a life of luxury.

Luci was hell bent, so to speak, on making sure that the later versions of Coach would properly "advise" customers representing each one of the "seven deadly sins." She personally had toyed with good examples of gluttony, lust, and greed, and now had a good set of criteria for future software updates to corrupt those types automatically through Coach. Thus, Luci now set her sights on sloth. *Many people are lazy*, thought Luci, *but I want to find an example where the laziness is hurtful to others. My best candidates are the world's so-called ethnic "princes" or "princesses." How can I find them in the customer database? Once I have found him or her, how do I best promote hurt all around? The hurt should come easily once I can provide useful "advice."*

Luci first thought of looking for customers with no salary. If they could afford Coach, then they'd be kicking around with some money, despite a lack of employment. She'd find retirees, housewives, and the unemployed. Lots of "cats and dogs." Just for fun, she typed in:
QUERY salary=0

The response came back:
OVER 500 RESULTS. PLEASE REFINE SEARCH.

I expected that, I guess. What if I refine the search by looking at their recent Web searches? Maybe I could find some candidates who were unemployed but looking for help around the house? Worth a try...

QUERY salary=0 AND searchword=cleaning service

244 RESULTS, PRINT?

Nope. Too many here. Let's try unemployed plus looking for a chef:
QUERY salary=0 AND (searchword=chef OR searchword=cook)

13 RESULTS, PRINT?

Why not? I have some time. Luci printed the thirteen profile records and studied each of them.

There are a few possibilities here. The best one seems to be Chandra Razdan. Let me open the complete profile... Luci highlighted the record of Chandra Razdan and hit "VIEW."

This is the one! Now how do I approach Chandra? I think the "analyst approach" might work well. Here goes.
Hello, Chandra. I'm Elsie from Eden here. Can u talk?

Chandra was caught off guard, but she replied.
Er, yes. Is there a problem with my Coach?

Not at all. I'm an Eden analyst working on the requirements for the next release of Coach. Do you have five minutes or less? I can call you back later if you like.

No, I can talk now.

OK. Calling...

Luci started her next project. "Hello again. My name is

Elsie. May I call you Chandra?"

"Sure"

"Well, Chandra, the next release of Coach will have the capability to work with you on your dreams and fantasies. All you would need to do is hit the 'dreams and fantasies' button, then select a category like 'living comfortably.' At that point, you could either type or speak into the microphone. We'd make sure that we'd help you fulfill all of your dreams. Is this a feature you would use?"

"Yes! I've been using Coach to look for a good cook and housekeeper. I've gotten some good responses. I just need to get their references. Would the new feature be able to help me with that kind of a search? I need to be a bit careful in spending my husband's money, so what if I wanted to find the best deal on a new Mercedes coupe? Would the new Coach feature do that?"

"I'll make sure it does, Chandra. It's coming soon, so watch for the upgrade notice. It will also be able to give accurate financial advice, so that you could invest your husband's money and then have your own to spend. You would just have to hook in his bank account number. Would you find that helpful too?"

"I'm not sure. That sounds like it might take up some of my time."

"Not at all, Chandra. All you have to do is put in the bank account number, and Coach will do the rest. It has access to all the top investment firms. It will automatically open up an account for you and put in it all of the profits, which you can then spend however you want. You don't have to worry, all the transactions are very secure."

"Wow! Thanks, Elsie. I can hardly wait. Thank you!"

"Thank YOU, Chandra, and have a nice day. Be sure to

keep an eye out for that update." Luci had hooked another one. She set a flag on Chandra's record to "MONITOR." She would monitor all of Chandra's future requests and intervene at just the right point. Soon Lizzy Silver would have a new investor for her Ponzi scheme.

Chandra Chopra had a match
And she would soon betroth.
She'd lounge around,

Detective Jim Kirkland sat in his one bedroom condo apartment, powered on his PlayStation 3 and took a sip of his beer. He needed to wind down. It was Sunday after all, and he had lost at least one weekend investigating that Billy Wilson death. That had been such a bust. The only thing the lab had gotten from the guy's SIM was that the device had been reloaded at 11:23pm, which matched closely with the time of death. Well, he could forget all about that now and play his video game. *Man, Suzie never accepted my playing these games,* he thought. *I kept telling here that it relieved stress, and also helped me prepare for any life and death struggles I might have in the future. Well, at least I'm finally going to get some uninterrupted time playing, 'Assassin's Creed III'. I waited for MONTHS for this to come out!*

He picked up where he had left off last night. He looked at his next mission, and sent his avatar in that direction, running along the tree branches and jumping from tree to tree. It was just like Parkour, or free running, that he used to do with his buddies, only better. He could leap and roll and swing every which way as he headed towards his next objective.

As he got closer, he slowed his character down. There were four British enemy soldiers just ahead. He crouched down on the tree branch and listened to the rhythm of the snare drum as they approached. As they passed by underneath his branch, he pulled out his rope dart weapon.

He threw it down into one of the soldiers, the dart piercing him and the rope wrapping around his neck. As he yanked the soldier up toward the branch via the rope, Jim slid down the opposite end of it, landing behind the other three soldiers. The three soldiers turned and one of the soldiers came up to engage him in hand-to-hand combat as the other two soldiers took aim at him with their muskets. Jim reached out and grabbed the soldier coming at him and turned him around and held him in front as a human shield. The other two dumb British soldiers opened fire, peppering their comrade with shot.

This is great, thought Jim. *I never get to do fun stuff like this while out on a case. Two down, two to go.* He dropped the dead soldier and ran up to the other two, pulling out and waving his tomahawk. As he neared, both remaining soldiers simultaneously jabbed at him with their bayonets. *Oh YES*, thought Jim. *Time for a double assassination!* He blocked one bayonet thrust and knocked that fellow to the ground while twirling and blocking the other thrust in one fluid motion. Continuing his spin, he tomahawked the same soldier in the head. As the dying soldier fell, Jim grabbed him and pulled him in between himself and the last soldier who was still on the ground. That soldier in desperation fired once again, shooting into his buddy. *Those guys just never learn, do they?* As he dropped his dead human shield to its knees, he leaped high over the body, raising his bloody hatchet, and brought it down on the last soldier's skull. Victory! Jim stripped the bodies of the few British pounds the soldiers were carrying and counted his loot.

Brinnggg, brinnggg.

Jim pressed 'start' to pause the game. He looked at his caller-id. It was the precinct. *Oh great, no rest for the weary. At least they didn't call in the middle of that fine kill.* "Kirkland," he answered.

"Jim, it's Captain Macfee. I need you and your partner to get on something first thing Monday morning."

"Why are you calling me instead of Tony? As the senior detective, he usually sets up what we do next."

"Because I'm your super sensitive Captain who takes care of all his little ducklings' petty needs, that's why!" said the Captain in a sarcastic tone. "And besides, Tony's wife flips out if I call their home on Sunday. She somehow got hold of my wife's number and now gives her grief eight ways to Sunday if I give them so much as a peep at home. So you get the call."

"Oh, all right. What gives?"

"I talked just now to a Sergeant Kevin Collins of the San Francisco Northern Station. He's investigating the death of the CEO of a company called ECS. They reported it as an accident to the press, but there were a few suspicious pieces of evidence at the scene. The fellow got crispy crittered in his private fire pit and there was a suspicious hole poked in the pipe causing a leak and the conflagration. They called me a few weeks ago to help investigate, but I nixed that since they didn't have any real evidence. Well, it now looks like they've discovered something new. Even though the top half of the guy was pretty well charred, they just found a partially burned note in his pants pocket saying that a woman called Luci, at his company, should be investigated by the police. They had a snafu where the clothes were peeled off for the autopsy without being properly searched, and they just found the note. Since the company's locale is in our jurisdiction, I need you and Tony to contact this sergeant and then get over there and find out more about this Luci woman's involvement."

"Ok, Cap. I'll make sure we get on it first thing."

"Good. Report back to me whatever you find out right away. If this new evidence leaks out to the press, I'll have them breathing down my neck for details and I'll need time to prepare a statement. Don't screw this up, Jim!"

The line went dead as the captain hung up. *Yeah, right,* thought Jim. *Everything's a crisis.*

He pressed pause on his PlayStation 3 to get back to the game, and looked at the three dead British soldiers with the fourth hanging choked from the rope. *No match for the mighty Jimbo,* he thought as he hurtled along the ground this time, bouncing over rocks and zigzagging to his next objective.

19 THE SERPENT AND THE MEDIA

One month after Sam's death, Coach 3.0 was released. Diane did a good job of seeding the marketplace and generating a "buzz." Much to her dismay, it turned out that Luci was correct in insisting that "sex sells." The sultry image of the "temporary" ECS CEO holding a martini glass and uttering, "What's your pleasure?" was a huge hit. Sales were brisk, and there was every expectation that ECS would soon be profitable for the first time this quarter.

Rose Chen had done her part too. All the sales channels were stocked, primed, and ready to go. When the gavel hit at 9:00 Monday morning, there were long lines outside of the major retail outlets.

It goes without saying that Ian and his development team exceeded all expectations. Coach 3.0 sailed through alpha and beta testing with only a few bugs, all of them easily resolved.

The media coverage was intense. If Luci's game plan was to stir up controversy in order to stimulate coverage, she was highly successful. The arguments pro and con Coach 3.0 were articulated in the press, talk radio, and television. All of this led to Luci's scheduled interview with Kim Lee on CNN Primetime. CNN Anchor Kim Lee started the interview.

"Good evening, Ms. Ferguson. Thank you for joining us."

Luci Ferguson, clad in a smart gray business suit and smiling broadly, sat across a square glass table from Kim. Her legs were crossed, as were Kim's. "Please call me Luci, Kim. I'm really happy to be here on your show. This is my first and only TV appearance, you know."

Kim turned serious for a moment. "Very much

appreciated, Luci. Before we get started, I need to tell you a story. I was hoping to learn more about your background and even invite some of your college friends from the University of Kentucky. When I started digging, I could find nothing about you. I called the university. I searched the Web and the social media sites. I…"

Luci managed her most polite smile as she interrupted Kim. "That's easily explained. The University of Kentucky had a fire in the Administration Building in 2001. My records probably were destroyed in the fire.

As to my lack of presence on the Web, I'm really a loner and have been all my life. While I understand social media well and value the role that it plays in the lives of many, I have NO time for it in MY life. My life is Eden, plain and simple."

Kim paused for a moment. Should she mention that she had searched for her family's "Ferguson" records in Ireland's www.rootsireland.ie site, finding nothing? She'd probably have a quick answer for that too. *Better move on*, she thought. She continued on to the next topic. "Makes sense, I guess. You're still a bit of a paradox…. Let's talk about the circumstances around your joining ECS…"

"OK. I was the largest investor in the very earliest days of Eden. I believed in the management and I believed in the Coach product. When I saw that they were heading in the wrong direction, I moved to California and joined the team. I increased my funding. I became the majority shareholder and I took control of the development plans. The Eden management team just needed a little 'tweak' as it were. They are finally back on track."

Kim continued. "And on track they are! Your recent success is truly remarkable. Besides your 'tweaking' the product's requirements, what other changes have you brought to ECS?"

"Rewards. The entire staff is highly motivated. I've rewarded each and every member of the Executive Board with additional Eden shares and other perks. For instance, when our Vice-President of Sales drives in tomorrow morning, she'll see a brand new Mercedes in her parking spot. I hope you're watching this, Rose!"

Kim had been waiting for the juicy parts of the interview. Now was the time. "Very good! I'd like to ask you now about the media attention brought to Coach 3.0 by the outrageous image of you quoting your new slogan 'What's your pleasure?' Whatever prompted you to do that? It was very 'un-CEO-like!'"

Luci was ready. "I'd do ANYTHING to boost sales. My staff liked the slogan and the visual that went with it. Why not? It worked, right? Sex sells!"

Kim almost fell back in her chair. She did not expect Luci's level of honesty. *Hmm. On to the next spicy one...* "Speaking of your staff. They were handpicked by the ECS founder Sam Washburn. And then came his tragic death. How did you feel when you heard the news?"

"I was devastated. We closed shop for two days. I'm still saddened by what happened that terrible day. Sam and I were very close from the day that we met until the day he died. He had an amazing mind and he was a good, thoughtful man. He must be looking down at us right now from wherever he is with great amazement at where I have taken his genius."

"It must have been quite a shock for all of you. My condolences." Kim was now quite ready for the conclusion of the interview. She had never forewarned Luci about what she had in store for her. "Before the next break, I'd like to have you meet Pastor Isaac White, of the Southeast Virginia Evangelical Church. As you may know, he has been highly critical of Coach 3.0 and has held many press conferences in which he called Coach 'the work of the devil.' Pastor Isaac?"

Pastor Isaac appeared next on the split-screen. A large, muscular African American with graying hair, he was sitting at his desk, behind which was a bookcase overflowing with Bibles and Christian literature. Not many people remembered him as a former pro football linebacker. "Thank you, Kim. And, Luci, I am happy to finally meet you."

Luci did not respond. For once, she was at a loss for words. *Let me just hear what he has to say,* she thought.

So Pastor Isaac went on... "We cannot tolerate a carefully programmed device which does nothing but lead people into vices of every conceivable form. The seven choices on your menu of 'dreams and fantasies' correspond precisely to the 'Seven Deadly Sins!' What in the world are you and ECS up to? You are in a position to undo centuries of good work by the Church!"

Luci thought quickly. *I could get into a debate now, but would that help any? It might just give this jerk a platform to further his cause. I might help sales a great deal more if I just walk off.* Luci pretended to get a phone call on her Coach... "Sorry Pastor Isaac and Kim. I have an urgent call and need to fly back to headquarters. Thank you for your time." Luci quickly walked off the stage and Kim called for a commercial break.

As it turned out, Luci's rapid exit from Kim Lee's show on CNN was the perfect tactic. The rapid sales path of Coach 3.0 accelerated further with the free publicity that started immediately after Kim's show and continued for three days, until the public got tired of the CNN flashbacks and the media focus turned once again to the Middle East. During the three-day media blitz, every news show on every channel repeated the last minutes of Kim's interview. Questions kept being repeated: Did Luci really have an urgent phone call or was she simply avoiding the questioning by Pastor Isaac? After two days, Luci had responded to Kim with the following statement:

"My apologies to Kim Lee, to CNN, and to the CNN viewers for making an abrupt exit from her show. I really needed to return immediately to ECS headquarters, as there were reports of a police inquiry into Sam Washburn's death. I would be happy to return to CNN at some future time, should I be invited. I would also welcome a serious debate with Pastor Isaac White at that time."

As it turned out, Pastor Isaac did return briefly to Kim Lee's show and said a few words. Luci Ferguson had declined the invitation to join him.

Consumers Reports Follow Up: "You wished and they listened. Six months ago we subjected Coach 1.0 to exhaustive user testing and found it to be quite innovative, but with enough deficiencies that it was not yet ready for the mass market. However, we have reversed our opinion after our latest testing with the beta code for Coach 3.0, which has now been released to the public.

There has been a dramatic improvement in this ECS product's 'wow' factor, due to a number of avant-garde enhancements. The smartphone has been updated to understand you much better through a short and easy to use interview section. Your resulting profile is then categorized into seven 'buckets', which seem to include pretty much any human indulgence you wish to pursue. It even taps your emails and phone calls to understand you better, though we were frankly a bit puzzled by the 'confessions' section. But not to worry, your resulting profile is encrypted with state-of-the-art techniques to protect your privacy.

Luci Ferguson, interim CEO of ECS, provided the following statement: "We have a very fervent crowd of early adopters who wished for a number of improvements, and we listened. They are so happy with the latest version that we have changed our slogan to 'What's your pleasure.'"

And a pleasure it was according to our testers. We literally had to pry it out of their hands and forbid them from taking it home. ECS has stated that the update is currently being rolled out to users, but you can download it immediately   at http://www.whatsyourpleasuresayscoach.com"

Luci called Ian into her office. "Ian, as I've said in the past, I've been doing a lot of hands-on with Coach and looking at user profiles. I've engaged a number of our early adopters to better learn how Coach can wow them. As a result, I have a good handle on how Coach can respond quickly to their wishes in a number of our profile segments. I want you to issue a software update that provides Coach with these new responses."

"Really, Luci? The whole idea of Coach was to find the best current answers for each user by mining expert databases and the Internet."

"Yes, you are correct, Ian. But remember our earlier discussion; computer learning is too slow and gets stuck at local maximum solutions. Now that we have those seven profile segments, we can input real-life best responses for each as a starting point. We don't have to wait for Coach to slowly learn for each individual. It can hit the wow factor with users almost immediately. It's similar to what developers learned in the computer speech recognition arena."

"I'm not familiar with that, Luci. What are you talking about?"

"Computer speech recognition does a lot of its work by

recognizing the patterns of words in a sentence. It knows 'two o'clock' is not 'too o'clock' because 'too' never appears before 'o'clock.' It has millions of these patterns. But the patterns built into the software don't work well in certain specialized areas."

"How so?"

"Here's an example. A machine manufacturer used speech recognition for the people who wrote their maintenance manuals. These people actually do the actions for a maintenance step, put down their tools, and then type the step in, and then pick up their tools and do another step. But by using speech recognition, they could just say the maintenance steps as they were performing the actions. It would tremendously improve productivity except for one thing. The users all got frustrated because saying something like, 'Apply molybdenum grease to screw threads and insert in slot B,' came out as gobbledygook on the computer. After a few sentences like that, the users gave up."

"So how did they fix that?"

"They spent an hour training the speech recognition system on all of their special maintenance words and sentences, and then distributed that profile to all of the users as a starter set. Then, the first time they used the system, it had 100% word recognition."

Ian suddenly perked up. "Oh, I see. So we're going to send out a starter set of responses for each profile. Great idea! And because of how Coach works, it will go from there to learn even more from each user to refine its responses to any quirks he or she might have. I like it!"

"Great. Here are compressed profiles for our first and seventh segments called 'Acquiring Wealth' and 'Eating and Drinking.' Send it out immediately as a 3.0.1 update. Users will just die for it!" Luci said with a maniacal laugh.

Well, that was a bit weird, Ian thought, *but she sure knows her stuff.* "Sure, Luci, I'll get it out today."

20 PEEK-A-BOO, I SEE YOU

Eric had tried following the young blond girl for two weeks now, but had only spotted her intermittently. In spite of his best efforts, he had yet to figure out how to get enough information about her to have a plausible excuse to call Elsie at ECS. As he circled his car around her favorite haunts, he spotted her and another girl going into the local movie theater. He quickly parked and followed them inside, just in time to get behind them in line to buy tickets.

"Two for 'Breaking Dawn-Part 2,'" said the brown haired girl.

"That'll be $15 for the 3pm in Theater 3," said the teenager behind the counter. The girl paid him, and then she and the blond girl ran squealing into the lobby.

Oh, Gawd, I should have guessed they would go to that one, thought Eric. He walked up to the counter. "One for 'Breaking Dawn' at 3pm." He paid, and saw that the girls were at the concession stand. He walked up behind them. *Oh, they are so cute. If only I could get a little closer and brush up against them. What excuse can I make? No, I have to be patient. I still need more information first. Arghh! Well, a little bit can't hurt.* "Excuse me," he said as he reached past the blond girl and grabbed some napkins from the dispenser. As he did so, he rubbed past her side briefly and smelled her perfume. He almost swooned from being so close to her. The girls were so busy deciding on what to get that they hadn't even noticed.

"Goobers, a small popcorn and a Coke," said the blond girl.

"Emily, get a large one. We can share, and after waiting ten months for Part 2 to come out, I'm so excited I could probably eat the whole thing myself!" said the brown haired girl.

"OK, but don't touch my Goobers! Let's go!" The blond girl paid and the two girls practically ran to hand in their tickets.

Eric ordered himself some Raisinets. *Oh, I'll touch your Goobers, all right, Emily,* he thought. He paid for his snack, walked over and handed in his ticket, and then walked into the movie theater. They hadn't turned down the lights yet, so he saw the two girls easily. He walked up the aisle, turned into the tier behind the girls and parked himself just off to the side of Emily. He listened as they both had their cell phones out and were talking:

"Jessica, text Trisha that she should have come. She'll be so jealous! Her parents grounded her for sneaking out with Brandon, last night! Lauren told me all about it."

"Oh, good idea, Emily. That'll get the bitch! She stole Brandon right away from you."

"I can't believe he went out with her. I'm going to find myself an older boyfriend, someone in college. That'll fix him. My sister Megan will find someone for me. I'll text her right now!"

Oh this is perfect. Her name is Emily; she has a sister in college named Megan, a friend called Jessica, and an ex-boyfriend by the name of Brandon. Eric got up and went into the lobby Men's room. He texted Elsie at ECS:

Hi, Elsie. This is Eric. I'm finally ready to take you up on your offer to help me track a friend. Are you free to call me?

Luci was sitting at her desk at ECS when up popped an instant message on her computer from Eric. She grinned and responded immediately:

Sure, Eric. I'm calling now.

Luci pressed a button which auto-dialed Eric's phone. "Hi, Eric. This is Elsie. What's your pleasure today?"

"I have a friend of a friend that I need to track down. Apparently she's pretty upset and needs a shoulder to cry on. But I only have partial information. She's at a movie theater right now watching 'Breaking Dawn-Part 2'. Her name is Emily, has an older sister named Megan, a friend named Jessica and an ex-boyfriend named Brandon. I'd like to add her to my contacts and be able to find her."

"Hold on a minute. Let me do my magic," said Elsie. She pulled up Eric's GPS information, and then had his location display on a map on her screen. She then had the map indicate all the local businesses in his area. She saw that, indeed, Eric was at a movie theater. *The letch was probably sitting right behind her,* Elsie thought. *Kudos to him.*

Elsie then fired off a command to the ECS communication partners for the cell phones currently situated near Eric's GPS coordinates whose owners' names began with Emily. There were four.

"Eric, I've found 25 Emily's watching movies right now," Elsie lied, not wanting Eric to know that she knew exactly what he was up to. "I'll need a minute to correlate the other information."

Eric was excited. This was James Bond stuff if it really worked. He could follow Emily all around wherever she went. Then a thought struck him like lightning. *What if I told Emily that her sister Megan sent me? I could be the older boyfriend that her sister was setting her up with!* Eric was literally hopping from foot to foot as he held his Coach to his face and said, "OK, Elsie. I'm waiting."

Elsie issued a new command, this time to the ECS social media partners to check those four cell phone numbers for

Emily's who had a family member named Megan and a 'friends' list containing Brandon and Jessica. In ten seconds, up popped one of the phone numbers and the words: 'Emily Johnson, 16 years old, 125 Maple Avenue.' Elsie issued a command to load the phone number, name and address into Eric's Coach.

She also loaded a routine that she had built which would track the GPS location of Emily's phone, now that she had her number. When Eric asked Coach where Emily was, it would route a command through the ECS system to the appropriate communication partner, and then route the GPS location back to Eric using the beta code for the "Find Friends" app.

"Eric, I have good news for you. Her name is Emily Johnson, and I've loaded her phone number and address into your Friends and Contacts list in Coach. The next time you want to know where she is, just invoke the 'Find Friends' application. It should then come up with a map of the area, with you as a red dot and her as a green dot. Just use the two-finger pinch function to zoom in and out. You can try it now, if you'd like."

Eric was so excited he almost dropped his phone. He tapped the screen to get to the applications, and then tapped on the 'Find Friends' icon. In a few seconds a map appeared with two dots very close together. He almost fainted from joy.

"Elsie, it worked! Thank you, thank you, and thank you! This is wonderful."

"All in a day's work, Eric. You go have some fun now with your new toy, and let me know if you have any problems."

"Yes, I most certainly will," said Eric. "Goodbye, Elsie." He hung up and walked back out to his car. It was amazing. As he watched, the two dots on the screen slowly diverged.

As he was watching his device, he tripped on the curb, and collided into the side of a car parked near the theater.

Oops. I've got to be more careful, he thought. *No time now to get killed, just when I'm about to have the moment I've always dreamed of.* He turned off his phone and drove home. *I need to have something to eat and carefully plan my next move. No fooling around in the shower tonight. I have to save myself for Emily.*

Eric Kruger liked his girls;
He watched them on his street.
He'll track them down,
All over town,

21 BLOODHOUNDS

(CNN) – North American grocery stores have reported a puzzling 25% increase in the sales of snack foods, especially pies, for the 3rd quarter. As a result, Congressman Kucinich stated today at a special session of Congress, "…we are actually giving tax deductions out to big companies that go ahead and advertise and market products that contribute to childhood obesity. So what I'm doing is introducing a bill right now that would protect children's health by denying any deduction for advertising and marketing that's directed at children to promote the consumption of food at fast-food restaurants or of any kind of food that's of poor nutritional quality." In a related story, the largest waist size of Santa suits 40 years ago was 50 inches; today it is 76 inches. Retired military officials have also been in the news recently, stating that American have become too fat to fight.

###

Sergeant Kevin Collins from the San Francisco North Station had arranged to host a meeting with Detectives Jim Kirkland and Tony Magnini, both of the San Francisco Central Station. Kevin was going to discuss his findings from the Sam Washburn crime scene and ask for their help in his investigation. After their meeting, they were to drive to a pre-arranged meeting at ECS with three of their executives: Luci Ferguson, Rose Chen, and Diane Jones.

Kevin led the two detectives to a small glassed-in conference room. He sat them down and started the meeting. "Thanks for coming over guys. The ECS trip should be very interesting. I can't wait to meet Luci Ferguson. She's quite the celebrity!"

"And she ain't bad lookin'," added Jim. "What a pair of knockers."

"Come on, Jim. Let's keep this on a professional level,"

said a smiling Tony. "You're right, though. Bet she's great in bed."

Kevin got serious for a moment. "She's a piece of work, alright. Did you see her on CNN? I thought she left that pastor hanging in the breeze. Very clever."

Tony jumped in. "We watched the reruns of the clip. Can you imagine the free publicity they picked up?"

Kevin went to the whiteboard. "OK, guys. Let's focus." He wrote down "Hole in pipe," "Hole in hand," "Bear?" and "Investigate Luci." Here is what I know. It looks like a routine accident except for a few things. There were these weird footprints outside the front door. Large footprints. A bear or something. They were just near the front door and nowhere else. A bear bite might also explain a hole we found in the deceased's hand and the hole in the pipe that sent the fire out of control. Really strange.

And then there was this note. Let me read it to you. 'Call police to investigate Luci.' Just those oddball things. What do you think?"

"It could have been a bear, but the imprints are long gone with the rain that we had," said Tony. "Let's focus on the note. We'll kick off an investigation today. Interview, then run a background check…"

Kevin interrupted. "You know that Kim Lee on CNN tried a background check on Ms. Ferguson and got nowhere. Maybe there's something funny goin' on. We should look into any criminal history and her finances. See what dirt comes up. We gotta do our due diligence here."

And Jim added, "We'll need to see her quite a few times, perhaps. Get to know 'er real good!"

They all laughed and went to the patrol car.

After the police arrived at ECS, Luci's admin led them to the Board Room, where Luci awaited them. Luci was wearing the same gray business suit she had worn on CNN.

Detective Tony Magnini did the introductions and then started the interview. "Thank you for giving us your time, Ms. Ferguson. We know your time is valuable and we promise to keep it short. Do you know anything about the death of Mr. Washburn? Was he upset about anything when he went home? Anything that you could recall might be useful. We want to finalize our police report and put the case to rest."

Luci responded. "I can't think of anything unusual. We had a meeting the morning of his death. Nothing exciting. He went home and the next thing I recall was the news report of his death. We were all very shaken here. He was irreplaceable, you know."

"Think hard, Ms. Ferguson." said Tony. Did he mention anything about his private life? Any problems?"

"No. But leave your card and I'll call you if I think of anything." *These guys are bozos. I'll just string them along. They'll never find anything. They just want to close the case as an accidental death.*

"Thank you again," remarked Tony. "One last item. Could you have the personnel records for the top executives printed out for us by the time we leave? It will speed up our investigation and reduce the number of questions we have for everyone."

"Of course. They will be ready for you with my secretary out front. Just pick them up when you go."

"Sure. It's been a pleasure meeting you. Take care," and Luci made her exit.

Rose Chen entered the Board Room and Tony led the introductions once again. Tony kicked it off. "Thank you for your time, Ms. Chen. We're concluding our investigation into Mr. Washburn's death. We are assuming that it was an accidental death, but we want to tie up any loose ends. Can you recall anything unusual in Mr. Washburn's behavior in the days prior to his death? Was he upset about anything? Please think hard."

Rose thought a moment. "I thought you might ask something like this. I keep going back to the days before his death and nothing unusual was going on. The same business-related crap. Not a thing. I really liked Sam. We all liked him. Great man." Rose started to shed a tear.

"Let me ask you then about Ms Ferguson. Did everyone get along well with her? Was there any friction between Ms. Ferguson and Mr. Washburn?"

Rose welled up some more. "Luci takes great care of us. When you go outside, check my parking spot. Luci gave me a brand new Mercedes without even telling me in advance. That's the kind of person she is. She really cares for her staff. No friction. Certainly not with Mr. Washburn!"

Tony sensed that Rose was getting upset. "We won't keep you then. Please take my card and call me if you can think of anything."

Rose gave a forced smile and walked out.

The last interview was with Diane Jones. As she walked into the room, both Jim and Tony could tell that she was troubled. After the introductions, Tony initiated her interview. "Thank you for your time, Ms. Jones. As you may have heard we are winding down our investigation into Mr. Washburn's tragic death. All the evidence points to an accidental death, but we're crossing our 't's' and dotting our 'i's.' Any thought you might have about Mr. Washburn's mood prior to his death might be useful. Did he have relationship problems here or at home? Please think."

Diane started to sweat. *How in the world do I handle this? Do I just shut up? If I say anything it might be overheard. If I send an email it might be traced. Even a phone call. I'll play it by ear.* "I can't think of anything right now. Sam's death was really tough on all of us."

"Well let's talk about the ECS organization. Is there anything we should know about the organizational relationships? Any problems? How about Ms. Ferguson?"

Now I'm really on the spot. I need to have them investigate Luci, but how do I work it? Diane paused for a long time. She had trouble making eye contact with Tony and looked down at the glass table. Tony and Jim knew something was up. "I really can't think of a thing. Sorry."

Tony offered his card and then Diane grabbed his arm. "Thanks for your card. Here, let me walk you to your car."

Diane accompanied the three policemen to the car, then bumped Tony's arm and handed him a copy of the note Sam had left under her door "This was Sam's note to me the day he died," she said. The note read, "Luci is not what she seems. Her ideas for Coach will have dire consequences. See me in the morning when you get this."

When they were all in the car and on the way to the San Francisco North Station, Tony read the note to Jim and Kevin.

Jim said what they all were thinking. "Shit! What do we do now?"

22 SMOTHERED WITH KISSES

(Washington Post) – Las Vegas celebrates 79th anniversary of 'Repeal Day.' "No other city in the world would dare have a Repeal Day party and here we are celebrating it," former mayor Oscar Goodman said as he posed next to a bottle of Prohibition-era Boord's "Old Tom" gin found in a second floor wall of the historic post office and courthouse that is home to the Mob Museum. "In my opinion, it's the most important day in the history of our culture." Current mayor Carolyn Goodman reported a 35% increase in visitors to 'The Strip' for the quarter, and attributed it to the 'What happens here, stays here' marketing slogan. In related news, Atlantic City has seen a 40% jump in visitors for the same period.

###

After his shower, Eric made himself some mac & cheese and sat at his dining room table. He turned on Coach. *This is unbearable. I have to see where Emily is right now.* He brought up the 'Find Friends' app, and in a few seconds was looking at the green dot representing Emily. He zoomed in by spreading his two fingers on the display map. *Ah, it looks like she's over by the Starbucks a few miles away. I probably should go right now, before her sister Megan has a chance to text her. This could be my only shot at her. I can't believe how great this Coach works.*

Eric quickly thought of a plan. He would drive around near the Starbucks until she came out, introduce himself as 'Brian', bring along some nice sweet wine to get her drunk, find a place to park, have some hot loving action and then disappear and start over with a new 'friend.' *Maybe I could even get her to go to Vegas with me for a while before I ditch her! Now that would be something.*

He went to the fridge and took out a bottle of sweet Riesling and two plastic cups. He practically ran out to the car, staring at his Coach to make sure that Emily hadn't moved. He rubbed some mud on his license plates as a precaution before getting in and starting the car.

Soon Eric was cruising around near the Starbucks and spotted Emily leaving. He pulled up next to her.

"Excuse me. Are you Emily? I'm Brian. I know your sister Megan from college. She sent me because she said you texted her about a problem with your stupid boyfriend and needed a hand. How about you hop in to talk?"

Emily looked at 'Brian'. He looked CUTE! And, he said he knew Megan from college so he was a college man. And he had his own car! Boy, was Brandon ever going to be jealous when she flaunted this at him. All her friends would be super jealous too! "Sure, Brian," she said as she jumped into the passenger seat.

"So, who is this jerk boyfriend?" 'Brian' asked as he put the car in gear.

"Oh, he's a big loser. He's not even first string on the football team. Hey, there's a game tonight over by the school. Let's go over there so you can see for yourself." Emily figured that she could hang all over Brian and really give it to Brandon.

"Well, I'm not so sure. Is there a place we can park?"

"Yeah, there's tons of spots in the back of the school that no one every uses. We can go there."

"Perfect."

Ten minutes later, Eric and Emily were parked at the back of the school. Eric could hear the band and muted cheers off in the distance. It was nice and dark here. "Emily, I brought some wine to help relax. But I'm not sure you should have any."

"I'm old enough! I've snuck beer with my friends, smoked cigarettes and been to R-rated movies. I'm not just a little kid! I'm almost seventeen!"

"Well, then, let's celebrate goodbye to Brandon," said Eric with a smile. He poured them some wine, and after they had drunk it, poured some more for Emily.

"Megan didn't tell my how beautiful you are," crooned Eric. "I don't have a girlfriend right now, and you're great to be with." Eric snuggled up against Emily and gave her a kiss. Then he gave her another kiss. He kissed her over and over.

Soon, Eric had Emily's bra, shirt and panties off and they were going at it. He couldn't believe how great this was. He was going to call Luci right after this and tell her he WORSHIPPED her!

Then, out of the corner of his eye, Eric noticed a light and heard a ping. The damned bitch was looking at her cell phone, right in the middle of sex!

Emily screamed. "Get off me! Who are you?" She started slapping him and screaming hysterically.

"Wait, what's going on?" yelled Eric.

"Megan just texted me that she didn't know anyone she could send to me! You don't know her! Get away from me!" She screamed loudly again and again.

Suddenly, the car door flung open, and four large guys from the football team who had been heading for the locker room dragged Eric out of the car and pummeled him to the ground. Emily yelled, "Hold him, hold him, I'm calling 911!"

Eric realized that Emily must have picked this spot so that Brandon would see them as he came back from the game. He tried to get up, but all four of the football players held him down. In a few minutes, the police arrived and hauled him away.

###

Eric sat miserably in his cell cursing himself. *It was all this fiendish Coach's fault! I never would have done this on my own! Well, at least Luci said she would get me a good lawyer. She said she would help me. She'll explain how I wasn't really responsible for what I did.*

"Kruger, it's time for your work shift," the guard said as he unlocked the door.

Eric followed the guard down to the prison laundry facility. Luci had told him that, if he was on his best behavior and did some work here at the prison, he could expect leniency from the court. He figured it would also take his mind off his situation.

"Alright, Kruger. Here's your station. You have to wash and dry the towels in this bin here, and the uniforms in that bin on the right. When you're done, you fold and put them over there on the table."

Eric looked at the huge industrial washers and dryers. There were four of each, and another three prisoners were already working in the room. They stared at him as he grabbed some towels and threw them in a washer with some soap.

"Hey, Asmodeus. I think this is that guy who was messing with kids," said the big black guy at one of the dryers.

"Yeah, we don't like guys like him, do we, Three Dog. He gives us cons a bad name," said a huge white dude covered in tattoos. "Daddy-Dee, didn't you say that you had-ta take a whizz?"

"Yeah, right. Hey guard, I gotta go do my business."

"Fine, let's go," said the guard. "And I'm coming right back," he yelled over his shoulder as he walked away.

As soon as the guard was around the corner, Eric felt himself grabbed from behind. He was about to yell when the guy with the tattoos shoved some dirty socks in his mouth! He tried to kick, but the con holding him lifted him up and the tattoo guy hit him right in the solar plexus.

"Asmo, tie an undershirt around his neck, I'll tie his hands with another one and let's toss him in the dryer!" Daddy-Dee laughed.

"You got it, DD," Asmodeus said as he rolled up a white shirt and tied it around Eric's neck. "I got him, DD. You guard the door."

Eric felt himself lifted and thrown into the darkness of the dryer that had been running. The heat was unbearable. *How am I going to get out of here? I can't even scream! Ugh, and what's that horrible stench! It must be these dirty socks in my mouth. It's like the fires of hell in here, with, what do they call it? Oh, yeah, brimstone.*

The shirt around Eric's neck caught in the barrel of the dryer, tightening and cutting off his air completely. The other socks in the dryer tickled his face as he spun with them. It was like being smothered by hot disgustingly smelly kisses. As his vision faded, he could see out the front of the dryer the laughing face of Asmodeus going round and round and round.

Eric Kruger liked his girls;
He watched them on his street.
He'll track them down,
All over town,
Then die of smelly feet.

###

Later that night, an email was sent out: "Ian, here is a compressed profile update for segment five, 'Improving your love life.' Please get it out as Coach update 3.0.2. Luci."

23 THE CHAPTER ON REVELATION

Diane's pastor, Ted Johnson, was quite a biblical scholar. Additionally, he had studied comparative religions while in the seminary. He had known the Jones' family for quite a while and was a spiritual advisor to Diane, her parents, and her husband. An African American who always had a kind word for everyone, he sat at his desk while awaiting Diane Jones' visit. He sprang to his feet quickly when Diane entered his office.

"Good evening, Diane. Good to see you. I'm always glad when we get together, but your phone call seemed urgent. Please sit down and tell me what's going on."

Diane sat by Pastor Ted's desk. She seemed very anxious. "I'm really concerned about the management of my company and the direction in which it is being led. Did you see the CNN interview?"

Pastor Ted showed his deep concern. "Not only did I see it, but I also recorded it. I've watched it many times. You know what? I even called Pastor Isaac to find out what he knew or what he suspected."

"Now you really have my attention! What did he say?"

"He really believes that there are forces of evil at play. He's not sure if it's because of Luci Ferguson specifically. He is very worried about the influence of your Coach product on our spiritual lives. Maybe we should talk about Ms. Ferguson and your perspective?"

"Luci Fer..." Diane almost fainted. "Please get me a glass of water."

Pastor Ted tried to comfort Diane. "Here, take this. Are you OK? Just sit a minute..."

"I'm NOT OK! Did you hear what I just said? 'Lucifer!' Luci Ferguson, Lucifer. Could it be? Am I crazy?" Diane got up and started pacing.

"Calm down Diane. Let's look at the pieces. We know from the CNN interview that her background is fuzzy at best. We know that the product line has moved away from the spiritual world and into the world of darkness and temptation; just listen to Pastor Isaac! We know that Sam Washburn died mysteriously shortly after her arrival. What else?"

"I've always thought that she was calculating and deceitful. Maybe a liar. I have no proof, though. What in the world do we do?"

Pastor Ted mused. "It's not entirely impossible that Luci Ferguson is Lucifer or some creature from Hell. Look, here in Ezekiel 28:16 it says that Satan is a cherub. In Ezekiel, describing the Cherubim, 'As for the likeness of their faces, they four had the face of a man, and the face of a lion, on the right side: and they four had the face of an ox on the left side; they four also had the face of an eagle.' Then, later in Ezekiel 10 'And every one had four faces: the first face was the face of a cherub, and the second face was the face of a man, and the third the face of a lion, and the fourth the face of an eagle.' Obviously, in comparing the two chapters, we see that a cherub can morph in appearance.

And there's more. Here in 2 Corinthians 11 'And no marvel; for Satan himself is transformed into an angel of light.' There's plenty of proof in the scriptures that Satan, Lucifer or whatever we might call 'The Evil One' is capable of morphing into any form, maybe into your CEO."

Diane paced even faster. "Now I'm really scared. Scared for my life. What can I do? What can we do?"

"First off, let's pretend we never talked. Go into work,

business as usual. Put on a happy face. Play it cool with Luci. Don't let on that we have suspicions. Have you gone to the police?"

"On the QT," said Diane. "I handed them a note that Sam Washburn had slipped under my door. It said something like 'Luci is not what she appears to be' and 'Her plans might have dire consequences.'"

"Good work, Diane. We can't tell the cops anything about our suspicions. They'll think both of us crazy. Why don't you stay on top of them? Call them from your home on your home phone. Make sure they do a thorough background check. If they find nothing more than falsified documents, we may unfortunately be correct. If she's just a scam artist or a criminal, they'll find that out and prove us wrong. Sounds like a plan? Look - there's good advice from Ephesians 6: 'Put on the complete suit of armor from God that YOU may be able to stand firm against the machinations of the Devil; because we have a wrestling, not against blood and flesh, but against the governments, against the authorities, against the world rulers of this darkness, against the wicked spirit forces in the heavenly places. On this account take up the complete suit of armor from God, that YOU may be able to resist in the wicked day and, after YOU have done all things thoroughly, to stand firm.'

Even our Muslim friends have something to say before they read their holy Qur'an: 'Auzu billahi minash shaytan ir-rajeem' or 'I seek refuge with Allah from Satan, the accursed.'"

Pastor Ted grabbed Diane's hand. They lowered their eyes as Pastor Ted led them in prayer. "Dear Lord, please guide Diane through the next days and months. Give her the strength and the wisdom to persevere and make the correct decisions. We ask this in Jesus' name. Amen."

Diane gave Pastor Ted a big hug, then left for the door.

24 THE EYE OF THE NEEDLE

(CBS NEWS) – Special Report: Tracking Sex Offenders. It is a rising problem in California... dangerous and high-risk sex offenders on the loose. These are predators who've served time in prison and are now back in the community. Because sex offenders are likely to commit new crimes, they're required to wear GPS monitors, strapped to their ankles. The monitors keep track of their every move. However, recently local parole agents tell us that those ankle monitors are being cut off, or the sex offenders aren't bothering to show up to be fitted with one in the first place. When we interviewed the San Bernadino County Sheriff, she told us, "Because of a California law passed in October of 2011 to reduce prison overcrowding, we no longer arrest these parolees for cutting off monitors. I don't know where these guys learned about this, but it means that serious sex related crimes have increased recently."

###

By the time Detectives Magnini and Kirkland arrived back at their precinct office after the visit to ECS, it was almost noon. "Hey, look who finally beamed in from the Starship Enterprise," yelled out Sergeant Tim Grimes. "Did you meet any weird alien women while you were out?"

"Stow it, Tim. That joke's getting real old by now," said Jim. "We only met some normal American babes. And before you ask, no, none were green, unless you count green eyes." *I can't believe my old man named me James T. Kirkland. I've had to live with these stupid jokes all my life. I guess I should be thankful he didn't also give me the middle name Tiberius.*

"C'mon Jim, just ignore him. We have to do some research on this Luci Ferguson. The note that Ms. Jones gave us could have just meant that it was normal infighting among the executives, but it does seem to provide a motive to do more than just play musical chairs for the CEO spot. I'll look through the database for traffic infractions and get any public records on her, while you search the Internet for anything suspicious. You youngsters are better at that web surfing anyway."

"Yeah, yeah. While I'm at it, you want me to buy you one of those cell phones they advertise for seniors on late night TV that have big buttons and only do phone calls?"

"Funny. Just start, and let me know what you find."

Tony sat at his desk, opened up Ms. Ferguson's personnel jacket that he had picked up at her secretary's desk when they left, and decided to start with the DMV system. The Department of Motor Vehicles would let him find out a lot of personal information like the locations where she had lived, besides any traffic violations.

Hmm, that's funny. It says here that she went to college in Kentucky, but there is no record of her having a license there or anywhere else until just this year. It's like she just popped into existence.

Tony then logged into the National Crime Information Center (NCIC) database, and the Interstate Identification Index (III) files, which contain criminal records for all 50 states. *Well, she certainly has an immaculate record,* he thought. *There's nothing here on her either.*

Finally, Tony accessed the three credit bureaus, TransUnion, Experian and Equifax to see if he could spot anything in a top-level report. He was accessing the basic report similar to those identity theft-tracking programs you could buy from Discover and other credit cards for a monthly fee. This wasn't strictly according to protocol, but might prove interesting. *Hmm, now this is definitely strange. The report doesn't show anything. No loan inquiries or credit lines at all. What, did she pay cash for everything including her car and house?*

Boy, she must be loaded.

This is like searching for a needle in a haystack. That reminds me, what's that quote that Father Murphy says all the time? I think it's something about it being easier for a camel to go through the eye of a needle than a rich man to get into heaven. Ain't that the truth. Rich folks here in California sure seem to go all nutso eventually.

Tony peered over his monitor to look at his partner. "Jim, I'm coming up goose eggs over here. Have you found out anything?"

Jim leaned back in his chair and scratched his head. "I'm crapping out here too, Tony. It's like she didn't exist before this year. The only thing I found was a few stories from this year about her and the company."

"Great; just great. I guess one of us is going to have to go back out there."

"That Rose gal was kinda cute, and I think she was giving me the eye," Jim said with a mischievous grin. "I've been kinda lonely since Suzie left. Maybe I can head over there and smooth talk her into dishing out some more details on our Ms. Ferguson and the others."

"OK. And while you're there, see if you can get them to cough up some computer records – emails, accesses to the security systems, stuff like that."

"Sure. Hand me Rose's folder so I can give her a call."

25 SUFFER FOOLS GLADLY

"Knock, Knock," Jim said as he tapped on the open door to Rose's office. "I'm so glad you said that you were free when I called a little while ago, Ms. Chen."

"Your call was a bit unexpected, Detective Kirkland, and I don't have much time. I have to get all of the latest sales figures to Luci by tomorrow. But Sam's death was so awful, I want to help in any way I can. I'm still not certain why you came back."

"There were some anomalies in Mr. Washburn's death that I'm not at liberty to go into just yet, and that first visit was just to get some initial background on your company. It's strictly routine. And, well, this is a little embarrassing, but you seemed so nice that I was hoping for an excuse to see you again."

Rose blushed. "Really? Isn't it non-standard procedure to hit on a suspect, Detective Kirkland?"

"Please, call me Jim. And I seriously doubt that you could have been involved in anything underhanded; that's why I wanted to see you. Could we check in with your CEO that it's OK for you show me around, and then have you give me the grand tour?"

"OK, she's just down the hall."

Luci was busy on her computer when Jim and Rose arrived. She looked up. *What? It's one of those nosy detectives again*, she thought. *I guess I'll have to do as that stupid Bible says, "For ye suffer fools gladly, seeing ye yourselves are wise." I'll just to have to outsmart this dimwit.* She put on her sweetest smile. "Oh, Detective. How nice to see you again. What brings you back so soon? No problem, I hope?"

Jim still couldn't get over how great this lady looked. A man-eater, for sure. He had to break eye contact, since he was sure Rose was watching him. He briefly glanced around the office. "I'm just following protocol, Ma'am. It seems that Mr. Washburn's death had a few, shall we say, peculiarities, and we need to track down some additional details before we close out the case. Could you arrange for us to get Mr. Washburn's emails for the last month? We'd also like a list of his phone calls and any security logs that show access to his ID and cell phone.

By the way, may I please have a glass of water? I'm real thirsty after the drive."

Luci grimaced inwardly. *That could be awkward. But I'll just go along with it, and then fix it so he gets nothing It's a good thing he's not asking for other information. These guys could really do some damage if they had access to the other files.* "Why of course, Detective. I'll have Ian McIntyre, our VP of Development, pull those for you. It will take a while to get that level of detail, so it might be a couple of days. This is a very busy time for us, since we are in the midst of improving our system even further. Just contact him later in the week. Rose, why don't you take the detective down to see the server farm while I go tell Ian?

Luci poured Jim a glass of water and handed it to him.

As Rose and the detective walked down the hall, Luci could hear him ask her, just before their voices faded, "So, Rose, how did someone so young and pretty get to be a vice president?" A few minutes later and while Rose was not looking, Jim dumped out the water and placed the glass in a protective bag. *Got some fingerprints, I hope.*

Luci opened her desk drawer and grabbed a few items and put them in her purse. She liked to think that she was prepared for any eventuality. She walked over to Ian's office. "Ian, quick, I need you for a second. Come here."

Ian looked at her, and then got up and came over. He was getting used to immediately doing whatever she asked. Luci grabbed his hand and dragged him a few doors down to the executive washroom. She opened the door, pushed Ian in, and then walked in and locked the door behind her. "Ian, you've been a bad boy. You need to be punished for your sins," she said as she pulled out of her purse a pair of handcuffs and a whip. Ian just looked at her stunned. In a few seconds, she had him undressed and handcuffed to the overhead light. Then she stripped down. She had on a black garter belt and crotchless panties.

"Um, Luci, you're going to take it easy, aren't you?" Ian stammered.

"Oh, Ian, I know you better than you do. You're going to just beg for mercy," she said as she rubbed the whip up and down his body. Ian closed his eyes and waited.

Afterwards, their lovemaking had been amazing. Ian lay on the ground spent.

"Ian, honey, one more thing. Those nosy detectives want to get all of Sam's emails, phone calls and any security system accesses. We just can't have that getting into the wrong hands. We have a great technology here, and I don't want our intellectual property leaked out to any competitors. Just stall on getting back to them. In fact, I want you to delete all of my information and Sam's information. Then we'll just tell them there was a glitch when we updated our system and everything was lost."

"Luci, isn't that illegal?"

Luci's eyes blazed. "No, Ian. It is our own information. We can do with it as we please, and I don't want to have it get out. Take care of it."

Ian thought about this for a second. *You know, as great as this sex is, I'm getting a really creepy feeling about her. Maybe I should back up all this information somewhere safe. I'm positive she would throw me to the wolves in a second if I don't have some insurance. And I better not directly lie to her. I'm sure she'd know.* "Yes, Luci," Ian said meekly. "I'll certainly delete it all right away."

###

Jim started the drive back to North Station. *I can't wait to tell Tony I got Luci's fingerprints. I never let on that I would collect her prints. Bet they find something in the fingerprint database. I'm sure she's got a criminal record! What else could Washburn have meant in his note? Meanwhile, it's great making a call on those two gals. Maybe this will drag out and give me some more house calls. It's 'win-win' for Jimbo. If the fingerprints solve the case, I'm a hero. If they don't, more house calls...* He smiled and drove on.

###

Days later, Luci decided it was time for more of her antics; she needed a break from the humdrum daily affairs of Eden. *Time for a really juicy one*, thought Luci. *Let's do "wrath." Yes, wrath is perfect. We'll wreck one poor soul and take lots of others with him. "The multiplier effect!" Love it. Let's get to work!*

Luci scratched her head. *Maybe the best way is to gauge user sentiment. One of the beauties of our AI interface is that it can track users' emotions in all of the feeds from our social media partners.*

I've never tried this before. I think the sentiment range goes from minus five to plus five, where minus five is "very upset" and plus five is "elated."

Luci started the search by sentiment.
QUERY averagesentiment=-5.0

The response came back:
DATE RANGE REQUIRED. INVALID REQUEST.

Yeah, makes sense. I'll look in the last 30 days.
QUERY averagesentiment=-5.0 AND date<30days

0 RESULTS

I guess no one was that upset for that amount of time. I'll see if anyone was between level four and five for thirty days...

QUERY averagesentiment<-4.0 AND date<30days

5 RESULTS, PRINT?

This time I'll print out the profiles.

Luci ran to the printer. She grabbed the printout and studied each profile snapshot carefully. Hmm. *This first one is arguing with his sister over their inheritance... The seconds is a wife whose husband beat her again. Oh, how I love domestic violence... Another is a guy whose girlfriend dumped him... Now a secretary pissed at her boss... Ah, the last one here's a possibility - an Arab fired from his job. Let's see what he's been doing.* Luci opened Ajmal Taqi's profile.

This one looks real good. He's been searching for ways to make bombs, and then erasing the search history on his browser. Must be paranoid. Time to put on my superhero cape and lend him a hand.

Luci created a dummy email account "serverfarm@edencoachingsystems.com" and sent Ajmal an email.

"Subject: Coach Groups

Your Coach servers have found other individuals interested in 'bomb making'. Please respond to this automated message if you would like to contact them to develop a 'Coach Group.' We are actively attempting to connect people with similar interests.

Thank you."

There was no immediate response.

Later that night, Luci repeated the email and changed the subject line to "Please respond. Second attempt"

This time Ajmal responded with a terse note:
"Yes, please."

Got him, thought Luci. She entered a query:

QUERY   searchword=bomb-making   OR
searchword=bomb AND date<180days

14 RESULTS, PRINT?

Luci declined getting the printout. Instead, she looked at each profile carefully, selecting eight good Muslim candidates scattered across the United States. She gathered the names, phone numbers, links to their online profiles and Coach email addresses, and created a file. She then sent it to Ajmal with "Subject: Candidates for your Coach Group."

Luci could not help but laugh. *Ethnic profiling can sure come in handy!*

Ajmal could not believe the intelligence and power of his Coach. Before sending an email to the potential members of his private "Coach Group," he looked up the profile of each person on the list. They all looked promising except for one woman. He sent out the following email to each individually:

"I am a fellow Coach user and I am interested in starting a group to focus on concerns with U.S. policies in the Middle East. I would like very much to talk with you about the group and the charter members. Please respond to this email and provide me with the best times of day to call you. Please feel free to check out my online profile.

Your friend in a common objective,
Ajmal Taqi"

In the next three days, Ajmal received five responses. It was all coming together now.

Ajmal Taqi had a trade,
But then he lost his wage.
He'll get a bomb
To serve Islam

###

After many blood tests, a colonoscopy, and many scans, the news came back to John Doherty that he had intestinal cancer. John rarely had gone for checkups, and never had had a colonoscopy so, regrettably for John and Patty Doherty, the outlook was not good. He had a fifteen percent chance of living another two years, with heavy radiation and chemo treatments.

Patty and John held each other tenderly when they heard the news. They cried silently. Then, after an hour or so, Patty summoned all of her strength.

"You will not die, John. I will find you the best medical care in the United States. We'll beat this one, you and I. Don't worry, I'm in charge."

And so she was.

Patty had complete control.
She'd fix her husband's ills.
He will sustain

26 EDEN AND POP CULTURE

Luci decided it was time to take the marketing of Coach to the next level. No way would she trust her next idea to Diane. Besides, she had the perfect way to execute this. She looked through her contact list for Lee Woo Yeun, who was the CEO at Netslate, the gaming company in South Korea where she was still a hidden investor. She found the international number for him and dialed.

"Yoboseyo, Woo! This is Luci Ferguson calling from the States. How are things in the Land of the Morning Calm?"

"Yoboseyo, Ms. Ferguson. I have not heard from you for quite a while. We are doing quite well here. The media storm created by some of the most unfortunate incidents you were involved in has finally died down. So, how can I help one of our key investors?"

"Woo, I'm involved in a new device here named Coach by a company called Eden. Perhaps you have heard of it?"

"Oh, yes. My contacts here were most disappointed that you chose not to involve our country in the manufacturing of it."

"Maybe we can change that in the future, but I need your help right now. Remember that emergency fund I left in your most capable hands? I want you to tap into it for a small project I have in mind."

"And what should I do with this money?"

I want you to contact PSY, who created the 'Gangnam Style' music video. Did you know that it surpassed the online views of Justin Bieber's 'Baby' music video not too long ago, and received over one billion views on YouTube in only five months? I would like him to create a new one based on Coach's capabilities. I'm sending you a file you can share with him that lists the seven areas where Coach can improve people's lives. There should be enough in there for him to create some very interesting visuals. I want it ready in two weeks. Money is no object. I'll supplement the emergency fund if needed."

"He will want full license to do whatever he wants in the video. And do you realize that it most likely will be very decadent?" Woo Yeun replied.

"That will be fine. The more outrageous the better. I'm looking forward on seeing it released."

Two weeks later, PSY's new music video "What you please" hit the airwaves. It was an instant hit, with over 50 million views in one day. PSY had young nubile women dancing in schoolgirl outfits while he mimed using binoculars and pushing the specs in and out while ogling them. He had another segment with women using slot machines along all the walls where he mimed pulling on a 'one-armed bandit' while using a pitchfork to poke them in their derrieres. Instead of snow hitting him and two dancers in the face as in his past video, he had the young ladies dress as terrorists with bombs strapped to them while flames danced all around. Needless to say, binocular miming and pulling on a slot machine while dancing joined the horse riding meme from his previous video.

This was also the third week in which Saturday Night Live ran their popular "What's your pleasure?" skit. In each skit, a comedian would converse with a Coach-like device that, in turn, would grossly misinterpret the comedian's "dream and fantasy request" and send her or him in totally wrong directions. This "What's your pleasure?" segment was hilarious and vastly popular, with each SNL comedian taking turns as the hapless device user.

Coach 4.0 had been released just one week prior after a heavy ground swell of clever marketing tactics, centered around the "tracking friends" feature. Sales were through the roof and it was unclear whether the pop culture exposure was driving Coach sales or that the converse were true, with the popularity of Coach having a solid impact on pop culture. "What's your pleasure" had become as ubiquitous as AOL's "You've got mail."

USA Today ran a feature article in which it stated: "...Kudos to the team at ECS. They took their Coach product clearly to the next level with a human interface that defies description. You can speak to your Coach and ask, 'Where's mother?' and have it reply in seconds 'At the A&P on Main Street. Shall I call her?' The 'Find Friends' feature is very easy to use and extremely powerful.

Another subtler feature is what an ECS marketing spokesperson described as 'communication through quadrants.' As it was explained to us, the Coach determines over time if a user is visually oriented or verbally oriented. It also determines if the user communicates on an emotional plane or intellectual plane. These four factors determine the 'quadrant' through which Coach communicates to any given user. Our staff has never seen anything like this and sees it as a breakthrough in human-machine communication.

Coach 4.0, as was the case in the previous release, comes with the heavy baggage of media controversy. Where does this all lead? Are there going to be subtle sociological changes? We may not know the answers to these questions for years..."

Pastor Isaac White continued with his criticism of ECS and of Coach. He had one or two brief appearances on cable TV with CNN and other channels, but really never had a chance to reveal his innermost thoughts through the television medium. He had, however, a blog with over twenty thousand subscribers. His latest entry:

"Dear friends in Christ

With the release of Coach 4.0 I see some real dangers to society. You can 'Find Friends' now on Coach, but what does this mean? You can be a sexual predator tracking down your prey. You can be a stalker tracking some helpless soul. You can be a criminal seeing if anyone is at home. Yes, you can **sometimes** "opt-out" of making your GPS coordinates available but you cannot do so easily on every device. More often than not, your GPS coordinates are fed into the ECS infernal machinery and made available to all forms of criminals and deviants.

The other major change ECS parlayed into Coach 4.0 was giving it the ability to communicate at a more human level. It does make Coach much more 'user friendly', but in an insidious manner. I have to ask what they'll do next. Will they have the device speak in familiar voices? I am really frightened about what the future holds for ECS and for Coach.

I have tried personally to get airtime to share my concerns but, all too often, my attempts fall on deaf ears. Perhaps the media outlets derive too much advertising revenue from ECS?

Pray, my brethren, pray. Pray that this hellish device can arrive at a well-deserved extinction. And, yes, share this message with everyone you know."

Luci, a follower of Pastor Isaac's blog under a pseudonym, had to chuckle to herself. *Pastor Isaac has just given me the next major feature of Release 5.0 - Text-to-speech with a speech model created for a fee. What a moneymaker! We could sell standard voice models of icons such as Marilyn Monroe, Frank Sinatra or JFK... We could, for a higher price, create voice models from friends' or relatives' recordings... Thank you, Pastor! I'll go have a late night meeting with Ian.*

Just after her rendezvous with Ian, Luci sat down at her computer sipping a glass of wine. She was totally relaxed. Things were going well, now that Coach was starting to corrupt people all by itself, so she had time to indulge in a little extra fun. *Let's see what I can write quickly. Hmmm. How about a small app like the Magic 8 Ball? So many silly beings just adore mystical advice. I know, I'll call it 'The Gypsy.' It will use the GPS function and the Watson back end to dispense advice on your current situation and the most immediate dangers you might face. Haha; that can't be all bad, right? I'll just tweak the twenty Magic 8 Ball answers to amp up the negative replies, and let Gypsy modify them if needed according to the answers it finds. There. That was easy. Now to submit the app. Fly my pretty, fly!*

27 INTERLUDE: THE GYPSY

Tim looked over at his lovely new bride, Suzie. Their Leonard's of Great Neck wedding was an hour behind them and had been a bit tacky, but the singing Elvis impersonator for the ceremony had been worth it.

"So, babe, what do you want to do first when we get to Montauk?"

Suzie just leaned back, laughing as her hair flew in the wind since the convertible's top was down. "I don't care, Tim. Whatever you want. This is so wonderful. My old boyfriend Jimmy would never have planned such an outrageous wedding. He just wanted to play video games and solve crimes. I was never going to get married at that rate."

"Yeah, his loss, babe. Say, how about we stop in that diner up ahead? I haven't gone into one of those old silvery things since my mom took me as a kid. They always have the best pie, you know. That's because everyone orders pie at a diner, so it is always freshly baked."

"Sure, Tim. Oh look, there's a spot to park right across the street from it."

Tim parked the car, went over to open the passenger side door and took Suzie's hand. They skipped into the diner across the street, ran to a booth and ordered pie and coffee.

While they were waiting, Tim pulled out his Coach device.

"What's that, Tim?"

"It's a new gadget than can do pretty much anything. It has a huge knowledge base. Watch. Coach, what is today's weather going to be?"

"Sunny, high 85 degrees, winds from the northeast at eight miles per hour."

"Ooh. Can it tell my fortune? I'm a Taurus."

"Coach. What is today's fortune for a Taurus?"

"There's a new application called 'The Gypsy' that will provide that information. Would you like me to download it?"

"Yes, download it now."

After a few seconds, Coach replied, "Download and installation complete. To invoke, simply say, 'Gypsy' followed by your request."

"Gypsy, what is today's fortune for a Taurus?"

"Reply hazy, try again."

"Tim, try it a different way."

"Yeah, yeah. Gypsy, what's in store for a Taurus today?"

"Better not tell you now."

Suzie felt a chill go up her spine. She hadn't told Tim this, but she was highly superstitious. "Tim, forget it. Let's just eat our pie and go."

"No. C'mon," Tim laughed. "Let me try another way. Gypsy, what should a Taurus be on the lookout for today?"

"Beware a stranger."

Johnny Esposito was driving around, trying to clear his

head. He was so unhappy at home. His wife was fat and dull. Their love life was non-existent. His neighbor, Raul, had everything that he ever wanted: a knockout wife, a beautiful house, a gorgeous expensive car and lots of friends. He just wished he could have that same life.

Johnny wasn't quite sure where he was at the moment as he pondered his current life. His Coach had the new GPS function, and he had told it to just give him directions for a pleasant drive. It pinged and gave him another set of directions.

"Johnny, turn left at the next light, and stop at the diner at the next corner. There is something you need to see."

Coach knew that Johnny was envious of others around him. It had profiled him by his usage into the 'Get what you want from others' category. It also knew via the GPS function that Tim and Suzie's convertible was parked by the diner.

As Johnny pulled up, Coach said, "Get out and look inside that Chrysler convertible on the street. Wouldn't you like one of those? It's much better than your junker. You could have a life worth living if you got one. Go into the diner and see what kinds of people own such a car."

From inside the diner looking out, Tim and Suzie saw a guy pull up and start walking around their car parked across the street and looking inside it.

"What the hell?" said Tim. "I'm going out and confront that jerk."

"No, Tim, don't. Ask 'The Gypsy' what we should do."

"Really? Ok, just for you, babe. Gypsy, should I confront that idiot outside?"

"Outlook not so good."

Suzie shuddered. "Tim, just stay here. He'll go away."

But Suzie was wrong. That stranger walked into the diner, and then started staring at them. Tim started to get up, but Suzie pulled his hand down. "No, just wait, Tim."

Sure enough, the stranger left after a few minutes, got in his car, and drove away. Suzie grabbed Tim's device and said, "Gypsy, will that stranger come back?"

"Most likely."

Suzie jumped in her seat. "Gypsy, should we leave now?" she asked.

"My sources say no."

"Gypsy, is our car safe? What could happen?"

"The Chrysler Sebring Convertible is the seventh most stolen luxury car in the United States."

"We've got to get out of here now!" screamed Suzie. She jumped up and ran out the door. Tim sprang in hot pursuit. As Suzie ran across the street, she didn't notice a large Hostess delivery truck filled with 'Devil Dogs' barreling down the road. The truck driver blared his horn as he saw the young girl stop right in front of him in fright.

Luckily for Suzie, the truck driver swerved, and Tim reached her just in time to pull her to safety.

"Suzie, what were you thinking? Come back into the diner."

As Tim and Suzie went into the diner and sat back down, Suzie wailed, "Gypsy told us that we shouldn't leave. It was right! Oh my God, give me that thing. Gypsy, is it safe to leave now?"

"Don't count on it."

"Suzie, this is ridiculous. I recognize those answers. They're just Magic 8 Ball answers. Let's pay and leave."

"No, Tim. That answer about our car being stolen and watching out for a stranger aren't standard answers. It KNOWS things! Gypsy, what's the fastest safe way for us to leave?"

"Concentrate and ask again."

"Gypsy, if we leave the car, can we get out of here safely?"

Coach noted that an Eden business partner ad for a car rental company was available. "There is a car rental establishment three doors down to your left. Rent a car. Run now. It is the safest option. Ask again tomorrow for further advice."

Suzie grabbed Tim's hand and dragged him to the car rental place. Soon they were miles away from the diner and their car.

Johnny's Coach pinged on the seat next to him as he was driving. "Johnny, I have updated information. That convertible that you saw is now an abandoned vehicle. If you would like to go back, I can provide instructions on how to hot wire it. You could have a luxury car of your own now."

Johnny shuddered as he reached over and turned off his Coach device. *I'm not that desperate yet*, he thought.

28 MIND MAPPING MAELSTROM

Patty and John Doherty lived with Lily, Patty's elderly mother. Two of their three sons also lived at home. One son, Sammy, was married and lived in a basement apartment with his wife and two children. The other son, Butch, lived upstairs in one of the four bedrooms. Both Sammy and Butch were unemployed and, to make matters worse, John was recently laid off at work for "health reasons." Sammy's wife, Linda, had a part-time job at a local insurance company but she had Crohn's Disease, worked only a couple of days a week, and brought in a limited income. All of this left Patty as the breadwinner for the entire household. No problem, as Patty had the inner strength to commute to her job in Minneapolis, take care of her husband, and run the household. If she ever got into trouble with her tasks, her two unemployed sons could help her with the logistics, or so she thought...

John Doherty had been getting progressively weaker and, as his cancer metastasized within his body, his wife Patty became more and more frustrated. She had been too busy to use her Coach for any use other than making phone calls, but that needed to change. Saving John was her top priority now and just maybe her Coach could help.

While at work and on lunch break, Patty had read about solving problems using "mind mapping," a planning process which solves a problem by radiating solution-oriented tactics out from a central problem definition. Maybe that's what she needed to help her organize her thoughts and focus more clearly. Patty went to the Coach app store and searched for "Mind Map." She found several apps, but the best-rated one sold for $9.99. Patty downloaded the MindfulMap app, paying for it with the credit card associated with her Coach account.

OK, the central problem is cancer treatment, thought Patty. She entered the words "cancer treatment" and the Coach came back with a display of possible tactics. She followed the branch that led to the selection of the best cancer care facilities; a listing of the top ten U.S. cancer care treatment facilities was displayed. *The best choice listed is the Anderson Center in Houston. This is clearly impractical, as I could not afford to take off from work and fly to Houston. The second best choice is Memorial Sloan Kettering in New York, again too far. Third choice: Johns Hopkins in Baltimore. Nope. The fourth choice could work - the Mayo Clinic in Rochester. It's a drive of more than two and a half hours from my home in Cambridge, but I gotta save John. I'll get a recommendation from our family doctor, Thomas Florentino in Minneapolis.*

Another suggested logic branch was "Finances." There were two forks off of this branch. One led to "Medical Insurance" and the other came to "State and Federal Aid." Patty considered the choices. *I have decent medical coverage for John and myself. Applying for state or federal aid will take too much time. I think we're OK here. Who cares about money anyway? It's all about saving John.*

Patty shifted the screen to follow a third major branch: "Support." One fork led to "State and Federal Resources." *No. This won't work either. I know so much more than any of those bureaucrats. John won't want a stranger in the house either. Not interested in getting this kind of help.*

Patty called her G.P. and set up a late afternoon appointment for next Monday. She then called Sammy at home. "Hello, Sammy. Would you kindly drive Daddy to Dr. Florentino next Monday? Our appointment is at 4:00 PM and I'll meet you there after work."

"I'm sorry, Mom. I have to take Linda to the doctor in the morning and Tyler has a soccer match in the afternoon. I'm an assistant coach, remember? Butch can't do it either. He's got a golf tournament."

"That's OK. I'll try my sister. See you later." She then

called her sister Carol. "Hi, Carol. Can you help me next Monday? I have to take John to Dr. Florentino. Could you pick John up and drive him to Florentino's office? I'd meet you there after work."

Carol thought for a moment. *My husband needs our car for work, but I can't use that as an excuse. I'll have to lie.* "We're both fighting the flu now. Maybe by Monday we'll be OK to drive to Minneapolis..."

Patty snapped back at Carol. "That's OK. I'll have to leave work early, that's all. I'll drive home, get John, and then drive to Minneapolis and back."

"But can't Butch or Sammy help?"

"Butch has a job interview and Sammy has to take Linda to the doctor. I tried them already. Goodbye and thanks for your help."

Bitch, thought Carol. She wondered why her sister had made the appointment first, without consulting anyone's schedules. *Oh well, she'll never learn...*

And so Patty was beginning to learn that the mind map for cancer treatment had many branches and many options. She'd have to examine each one, one by one. Some she would have to dismiss because she didn't have the time, and the others she'd have to take care of by herself. But her Coach and her MindfulMap app would guide her through the process. Yes, she was in charge again.

Patty had complete control.
She'd fix her husband's ills.
He will sustain
Despite the pain

29 O LE ALI'I ASO

Thanks to Luci's intervention, the Silvers were able to quickly round up twenty-six well-heeled new clients, clients very interested in a portfolio of Israeli tech startups. All the startups were legitimate. Lizzy and Fred had worked diligently, utilizing both phone and video conferencing, to create a quite impressive package for potential investors. While some of the business was conducted remotely, most of the clients were wined and dined at the Silvers' mansion in Greenwich. The story given to each and every investor was the same: These were legitimate Israeli startups with a great deal of potential. The money being raised as seed money would be delivered proportionally to each company during one comprehensive trip to Israel. The Silvers had raised well over twenty million dollars, depositing the money in a Swiss bank account. The only problem for the investors was that the Silvers were on an Hawaiian Airlines plane from Honolulu to Pago Pago and not on their way to Israel.

Fred was savoring his second glass of champagne on the flight. Lizzy was already on her fourth. He leaned over to Lizzy. "Hey, honey. Watch the booze. We still have a great deal of traveling to go."

Lizzy composed her somewhat disheveled self. "Yeah, yeah. I packed two bottles for our charter flight from Pago Pago to Matavai. Guess I'll hold off till then. By the way, are you sure that Samoa has no extradition treaty with the United States?"

"Double and triple checked it. I even made some calls to the government. No problem. We're finally going to be living our retirement dream, albeit a little earlier than planned. Let me ask you something now - where are we on your investigation into buying a resort property?"

"We have two set up on the north coast and one on the southeast sector. That should work for starters. Our first appointment is in two days that should give us enough time to settle in and do the tourist bit. Hey, I'd like to read to you a funny article I saved on my laptop while searching 'Samoa' on the Internet. Want to hear it?"

"Sure, hon. we've got the time."

"OK. It's a translation from the Robert Luis Stevenson Museum in Vailima, Apia. 'This is the story of the cannibalistic repast of king Malietoa. The chief's full name was Malietoa Uilamatu (Faiga). He was a cannibal and victims for his meals where provided from all over Samoa; the victim was euphemistically called "The Chief's Day."

Malietoa lived in a piece of land between Afega and Malie. It is known the Tualagi and was some distance inland from the main road. The king always had some hangers-on such as chiefs and orators, waiting in front of his house for the two victims he demanded daily from this or that village. When the poor fellows arrived, they where thanked by the reception committee, and committed to the young men to be dispatched and cooked.

There was a flat, smooth rock where the victim was placed to be killed before being taken to the cookhouse. There his arms where tied to his body and he was seated on the oven, legs folded under him, as if he were still alive. Thus he was roasted. When he was well done he was taken to the king's house and cut up. The king got the nape of the neck; the rest was distributed among the chiefs and orators, and the members of their families. It is not known now whether the intestines were eaten like those of the pig, but it is certain that the king got the heart.

The capital was always full of people because many strong and bold men from the different districts used to congregate there to protect the king. They all took part in the cannibalistic feasts.'"

Fred laughed heartily. "Good one, Lizzy. Our first appointment is at the museum to see The Chief, right?"

"Yeah. I hope he speaks English."

Lizzy Silver loved her gold,
But watched her wealth recede.
She'll get it back
With methods black

###

After arriving at their hotel in Pago Pago, the Silvers had both started and finished the two champagne bottles they had stowed in their luggage. The flight from Pago Pago on American Samoa to Matavai on Samoa would be quite short by comparison, so they could just settle in and enjoy the flight.

Fred and Lizzy had loaded their luggage and introduced themselves to the Samoan pilot, Jason Benga. The plane was a four-seater, with the pilot sitting in the front left seat and the Silvers occupying the two rear seats.

"Make yourselves comfortable," said Jason. "You guys seem tired. Go ahead and sleep, if you wish. We'll be flying through some small tropical storms, and we might hit some turbulence, but don't worry, you're in good hands!" Those words were the last English words they would ever hear.

###

Something jolted the plane, probably a lightning strike. The Silvers' charter flight crossed over the Apolima Strait and careened, out of control, into the jungles of Samoa.

###

Lizzy was the first to become conscious. She quickly surmised that they were on the ground; God knows where in the Samoan jungle. She noted that poor Jason had crashed through the windshield and was very dead. Still somewhat in a drunken stupor from the night before, she managed to splash water from her Poland Springs bottle into Fred's face. She shook his head and screamed. "Fred! Fred!" but he did not move.

Fred managed to respond weakly to Lizzy about two hours later. The two Silvers held each other and sobbed softly. They were both pinned down in the aircraft and could not move and, as night fell, they fell asleep.

With the dawn came excited voices from outside the plane. *Oh, thank God*, Lizzy thought. *They saw the plane come down and they've come to rescue us!* "Over here, over here!" shouted Lizzy.

She heard the voices repeating "O le ali'i aso! O le ali'i aso!" Lizzy had no idea what they were saying, but she was so very happy that help had arrived.

Five brown-skinned youths, clad only in loincloths, worked feverishly to pry open the aircraft's door. They then hastened to free both Lizzy and Fred. Although they were less than careful in their maneuvers, they were able to extricate the Silvers and tie them, using vines, to two makeshift stretchers made from tree branches. Lizzy mumbled to Fred that this was probably for their safekeeping while they were transported to a vehicle for transit to the local hospital. Fred agreed, and then dug into his wallet to offer the natives a payment for their services. He pulled out a one hundred dollar bill and handed it one of the youths, who looked at the money curiously, then proceeded to put it in his mouth. The native quickly grunted and spit it out.

After a long, arduous and painful journey, the natives brought the Silvers to a set of crude huts. *Must be their village*, thought Lizzy. *We'll be at the hospital in no time.*

Awaiting the five youths was the enormous chieftain. His face was painted with white stripes, and he was wearing at least seven ornate bone necklaces. Without saying a word, he pointed to an area to his right where several large pots were sitting on top of flaming embers.

After the five youths released the Silvers from the vines that held them to the stretchers, they picked up both Fred and Lizzy, carrying them to two of the awaiting pots. As Lizzy screamed "Shit no!" the boys ceremoniously slid the Silvers' bodies into the boiling oil in preparation for the Chief's Day feast. While Fred and Lizzy bubbled in the oil, the youths danced like demons around the two pots. They were chanting "O le ali'i aso! O le ali'i aso!" It meant "The Chief's Day."

Lizzy Silver loved her gold,
But watched her wealth recede.
She'll get it back
With methods black
But wind up as "chief feed."

Luci had trouble containing her excitement. Coach 4.0 sales far exceeded all expectations, her human "experiments" were yielding a new collection of souls and she, thanks to Pastor Isaac, had a brilliant idea for Coach 5.0. It was time for an evening meeting with Ian. Luci sauntered into Ian's office and closed the door.

"Hey friend. How do you like your new car?"

"Love it Luci. Thank you very much. It's not the one I would have chosen but it's much better than my Acura. To what do I owe this pleasure? You didn't bring the whip, I hope."

"Hah. Hell no. I want to share some very good news with you. First off, we could well afford your new Dodge Viper. Our sales are going like gangbusters and we have a large revenue stream from advertisers."

"Interesting. Any particular profile to the advertisers?"

"Not really, but the pattern is becoming clear. We charge a premium for our GPS location-based advertising and that, coupled with our 'communication by quadrant' is doing extremely well. We notify boozers that they are driving by a liquor store with sales on their favorite libation. We tell foodies about their favorite restaurants' 'daily specials' as they drive near. I even have a thank you letter here from the CEO of a car rental company who has received a few quite profitable emergency rentals recently. You get the picture."

"Nice. But I'm sure you had more on your mind, Luci."

Luci unbuttoned her blouse. "Well, I did. I subscribe to a number of blogs, as you know. One of them just gave me a great idea - text-to-speech voice modeling."

"Let me be sure I understand. You're talking about creating speech models for 'the voice of Coach' patterned after a particular person, right?"

"Exactly. We could charge for standard voices, like Marilyn Monroe, JFK, etc. We could also charge a significant fee for custom voices. I know that the technology exists to create voice models for speech recognition, but how about for text-to-speech. What's the latest?"

"A few labs are toying with this concept: AT&T, IBM, and Kurzweil. Nothing like this is ready for prime time yet and we certainly don't have the expertise here."

"Why can't you make some calls tomorrow to see what we can beg, borrow, or steal?" Meanwhile, let's celebrate your new car." Luci slipped out of her clothes again.

###

Ian made close to one hundred calls in the next week. As he was well known, even revered, within the technology space, he had no trouble reaching the right parties fairly quickly and assessing the text-to-speech landscape. He set up a morning meeting with Luci to go over his findings.

"Hey, Boss. Got some news."

Luci smiled and looked up from her keyboard. "Good news, I hope."

"Maybe yes. I found a guy, actually a friend of mine. He has what he claims is breakthrough software. It's in beta code now."

"Great! What do they want for it?"

"It's not that easy. He works for one of those big labs. I cannot even give you his name or where he works."

"Tell me more. Can I bribe him?"

"To tell you the truth, it happens that he is in big financial trouble. His wife caught him cheating and is suing him for divorce. It's going to be very ugly."

"Look, Ian. This code means a lot to me and to Eden. Write him a personal check for what he needs or wants and get the code. I'll reimburse you. Let me know if you need money in advance."

Ian struggled to answer, so Luci continued. "Ian, look. This guy is a friend in trouble, right? You'd be helping him out and giving us a 5.0 headliner. Win-win. What do you say?"

"Let me talk to him. No promises." Ian walked out of Luci's office thinking *Gawd, what will this broad pull next? She has no sense of ethics, business or otherwise. I'm not sure that I can even trust her. I love the sex, though…*

Two weeks later. Ian had a CD-ROM with his friend's beta code and Luci had what she needed for an early release of Coach 5.0.

A newscaster in American Samoa had written a story about Jason Benga's missing aircraft and the two missing American passengers, Fred and Elizabeth Silver. A New Zealand newspaper covered the story, and then it was picked up by Reuters and sent worldwide. It might have gone relatively unnoticed except for the fact that Allen Abraham, a reporter for the Wall Street Journal, happened to see the Reuters wire dispatch. By unhappy coincidence,

Allen was one of the twenty-six investors sucked in by the Silvers' Ponzi scheme.

Allen Abraham put two and two together, guessing that he and some number of others might well have been duped. He did, however, need to gather more facts. He called the FBI who put a small team on the case. Two weeks later, the FBI delivered a detailed report. The Silvers had apparently moved out of Greenwich, taking their two laptop computers with them. They had made no plans to travel to Israel, instead flying first to Pago Pago and then, by charter flight, to Samoa. The FBI had concluded that the Silvers had left the United States heavily in debt, moving to Samoa to avoid potential extradition. They had also concluded that Benga's plane had crashed during a storm and would not be found easily in Samoa's impenetrable jungle. They had no idea what happened to the funds that the Silvers had swindled.

Allen did next what he presumed to be the right thing: He wrote a detailed expose' of the Silvers and their Ponzi scheme, a story first picked up by the New York Times and then by all of the major media channels.

Raj came home from work to discuss his finances with Chandra. As soon as he opened the door and hung up his jacket, he looked for Chandra. Chandra was sitting in the kitchen, watching *The Dr. Oz Show* and eating potato chips.

Raj sat across the kitchen table. He seemed quite troubled. "We need to talk, Chandra."

"Could I just finish the show? It's about diet and cholesterol…"

"No, dear. This is serious. Please listen…"

Chandra turned off the TV. She looked over at Raj but

continued her munching. Raj went on with his story.

"Our checks are bouncing! I tried to transfer some funds from our personal account to the corporate account and found that there's nothing left. I called the bank, which informed me that you have been transferring money out. What's going on?"

"I don't know. My Coach device had invested our funds and said everything was going great. Here, look for yourself," Chandra said as she handed her Coach to her husband.

Raj examined the transactions in his wife's device. As he paged through the transfers, his amazement suddenly turned to horror. "Oh my God! It's invested everything in a set of Israeli startups. The funds were transferred to Silver Investments, but I just read in the paper this morning that Mr. and Mrs. Silver left the United States and were lost in a plane crash. I think they took our money with them. This is a disaster. I can't believe you let this all happen automatically. We're flat broke, Chandra."

"What does that mean for us?"

"I was about to fund some of the operations of my company from our account. With the recession, business is down and we're having a severe cash flow problem. To keep the company alive, we're going to have to downsize and you might have to take a job."

"Can't your parents send you money?"

"No, Chandra. It's not fair to them. I cannot ask them to bail us out for our risk-taking. Absolutely not."

"Well then, you're going to have to find a second job. Remember your wedding vow? 'I will always make an effort to ensure her comfort and happiness.'"

Raj could not believe what he was hearing. *I'll bet she'll also bring up 'I will never express dissatisfaction about any shortcomings in Chandra. If there are any, I will explain them to her lovingly. I will support her in overcoming them.' And 'I will not find fault or criticize Chandra before others. We will sort out our differences and mistakes in privacy by ourselves.' I'm a man of my word. I regret ever saying those words in front of a man of God. I'll bite my tongue and look for a second job. I wish she understood...* Raj could say nothing more. He walked out of the kitchen as Chandra was saying "Remember it's my Mah Jongg night, dear. I'll see you later tonight.

Chandra Chopra had a match
And she would soon betroth.
She'd lounge around,
A princess crowned

31 STUMPED

Detective Tony Magnini sat drinking his first cup of coffee; he called over to Detective Jim Kirkland. "Hey, Jim. Pull up a chair. Let's talk about the ECS case."

Jim poured his own coffee and sat next to Tony at the Central Station's kitchen table. "First off, Ferguson's fingerprint search yielded zippo. She's certainly not a known criminal. Also, I think she's stonewalling us. She won't answer my phone calls and it's been a couple of months since I asked her for the computer records. I don't think she plans to do anything whatsoever."

"So what's our next step? Do we just walk away? Should we get a subpoena? The note I got from Diane Jones was disturbing. I don't think we should drop the ball on this case. You were the last one up there. You know the politics a little better than I. What do you think?"

Jim thought a moment. "Why don't we invite Diane Jones to meet with us here? I suspect she'll welcome the opportunity to talk with us away from ECS Headquarters. I'll give her a call."

"Good plan, Jimbo. If this fails, I'll crank out a subpoena."

###

One week later, Diane drove into San Francisco and parked by the Central Police Station. Detectives Kirkland and Magnini quickly greeted her as she walked in the door. Tony shook Diane's hand and started the conversation. "Glad you could come, Ms. Jones..."

"Please call me Diane, Detective."

"OK then. I'm Tony and this is Jim. We'll work on a first

name basis. Follow me, please. We have a conference room."

Tony escorted Diane and Jim to a glass-walled conference room where there was a fresh pot of coffee, a pitcher of water, and some plastic cups.

"Anything to drink, Diane?" asked Tony.

"No, thanks. I'm all set. What's on your mind?"

"Well, You are on our mind. The note that you passed to me in the parking lot really piqued our interest. Quite frankly, we might have just walked away from the Washburn case thinking it was an accident had you not given us Sam's note.

Since that day, we have conducted a search with Ms. Ferguson's fingerprints. No criminal record. Also, there's not much on her anywhere: no motor vehicle records, no school records, nothing.

Jim called on Ms. Ferguson a couple of months ago and asked for ECS computer records. He has since followed up with a number of unanswered phone calls with requests for all the top executives' emails, phone records and security accesses. We strongly suspect that the ECS computer records will tell us something, but she's blocking our access. We have two choices: (1) Get a subpoena or (2) ask if you could get them for us on the QT. What do you think, Diane?"

"I can understand Luci's reluctance to help out. She might have even asked that all relevant records be deleted. Trouble is, she has a 'relationship' with our Ian, VP of Development and that could pose an additional problem in getting the information you need. What do you need specifically?"

"Your VP of Development might know better than we

do. We'd need just about everything in the week before Mr. Washburn's death and a couple of days afterwards. Security records, phone records, emails…"

"You're right. Ian would know better than any of us. I'll try to work on him, but no promises. I'll need to wait for the right opportunity."

"Thank you, Diane. Please contact either of us if you think we can help in any way. If we don't get anything from you in the next month we may need to get a subpoena. I'm sure ECS doesn't want that."

"Correct, Tony. Wish me luck."

The two detectives shook Diane's hand warmly and sent her on her way.

·

32 SHOCKED

The MindfulMap on her Coach was doing an amazing job of suggesting the paths that Patty should follow to get her husband the best possible treatment for his cancer. Following her Coach's suggestions, and armed with Dr. Florentino's referrals, she had lined up a quality surgeon and oncologist at the Mayo Clinic. Her immediate problem then became one of managing the logistics of all the recommendations from the mind mapping software. She also had to maintain her job in order to support Butch, Sammy, and Sammy's family living in the basement. She had to drive her husband John to Dr. Florentino, to the Mayo Clinic for tests, to the oncologist and to the surgeon. Her youngest son, though unemployed, was usually unavailable to help much with the driving - too busy ferrying his wife Linda to the E.R. Butch was of limited use, between playing golf and being heavily involved with his gambling habit. Her sister Carol was not available "on demand," as it were. And so, it was work a day, then back to the doctors, on to the tests ad infinitum. John Doherty was thinking, *I couldn't say anything to upset Patty. She's doing her best to keep me alive, but I just want to die in peace. Please God; help me to die in peace.*

The stress was getting to Patty. What started as tension headaches later became migraines. The migraines were soon augmented by a twitch over the eyes, then a full facial twitch. It was becoming unbearable, so much so that Patty lashed out at her mother, her sister, and her children - everyone but her husband.

###

About five weeks later, Patty lay strapped to the wheeled gurney, her head, arms and legs restrained, multiple electrodes attached to her head. Her left eyelid and leg twitched simultaneously. She looked up at Dr. Vijay Kumar.

"Get on with it already. I can't stand being like this another second!"

"Patience, Mrs. Doherty. We are almost ready to turn on the device. We need to finish the final diagnostic checks first. My assistant here will give you your shot, which will prepare you for the treatment." Patty looked at the assistant. *Wow, he seems so nice, and handsome too. I don't know why I was worried about some crazy nurse being here. This hunk could never do me any harm.*

This was Patty's second visit to Dr. Kumar. The therapy had worked splendidly the first time, but all of her symptoms had now returned. She thought back to how she had come here.

The twitching had started a few weeks previously. She was sure that this was from being overwhelmed with all the requirements of getting her husband the best care. It had reached the point where she could only get a few hours' sleep, and even driving had become dangerous. Finally she had asked Coach, "How do I stop twitches?"

Coach had responded that Electroconvulsive Therapy, or ECT, was the best option. "What?" she shouted at her device. "Have you started malfunctioning already, you confounded piece of electronic garbage? You're recommending shock therapy? That's what they gave crazy people ages go. I saw 'One Flew Over the Cuckoo's Nest.' That Nurse Ratched character gave me the creeps for a long time. I thought shock treatment had been banned after that."

Coach calmly gave her the facts. Part of the problem was that patients needed to be anesthetized before the seizure inducing therapy, and this tremendously reduced any adverse effects. Aberdeen University in Scotland had published a paper recently in the Proceedings of the National Academy of Sciences (PNAS) journal that helped doctors understand how ECT worked. They found that ECT appeared to turn down overactive connections between parts of the brain that control mood and parts that control thinking and concentrating. After the shocks were administered, patients' moods lifted and their brains settled down. The only side effects were mild forgetfulness and in rare cases retrograde amnesia. The symptoms disappeared after a short time.

Well, I guess a little forgetting for a while wouldn't be so bad. At least I'd stop twitching and get some sleep, she thought.

"OK, make me an appointment to see the nearest doctor who can take me immediately," she had told Coach.

Coach had searched through the extensive literature, contacted the schedules at various hospital computers, and found a doctor. Unlike Patty's other requests for information, where she received lists of recommendations and then decided on the best approach herself, in her harried and frazzled state she had issued a very specific request for the nearest and most available doctor. Like generations of computer programs before it, Coach answered the question directly without regard to what was best.

There were much better doctors available, but none that met all of Patty's stated criteria. Thus, Coach gave her Dr. Kumar's name, along with the additional information that he was highly popular on the Blogosphere, had an office only two miles away, and was free tomorrow. She had then told it to make the appointment.

What Coach had not discovered, or had not shared, was that Dr. Kumar was a slight quack, and his practice was very new. He also used sedation instead of anesthesia, and his assistant was addicted to pain medications and had been slowly replacing the medications with plain water.

###

"The checks are done, Mrs. Doherty. The shot should have you prepared by now. Are you feeling calm and relaxed?"

"Yeah, yeah, I'm great. Just do it already. Can't you see I'm still twitching? I need you to get a move on. I have lots to do today."

Doctor Kumar turned towards his assistant. "Set the device for one quarter power to start."

The assistant did as he was told, and then pushed the 'engage treatment' button.

Patty felt a jolt, and then a bit of euphoria. *Ahh, this is great. I even forgot about what I have to do after this for a second. And my eyelid and leg have stopped twitching already.* "Do it again, Doctor. It's working!"

Dr. Kumar nodded towards his assistant, who pushed the engage button again. Suddenly, sparks started flying out along the whole face of the device. All of the wheel-like dials turned towards their maximum stops.

Patty felt her whole body turn rigid, as if she had stuck her finger into an electric socket. A light show was flashing all across her retinas. It felt like Lucifer was pouring waves of hot lava up and down her body. She did not see the smoke coming off her head where the electrodes were attached.

The assistant was frantically pushing the 'stop' button and yelling, "What should I do? I can't turn it off!"

Dr. Kumar rushed over to the machine and yanked out the power cord. He looked over at Patty. She was lying there with her eyes rolled up, only the whites showing, smoke slowly wafting towards the ceiling. He went over and patted her on the cheek. "Mrs. Doherty? Mrs. Doherty?"

###

Patty's husband, John, sat in his wheelchair looking sadly at his wife. She just lay there deathly still, not moving, with her eyes staring up at the ceiling.

Dr. Kumar was squeezing his shoulder. "We did everything we could. No one could have foreseen this. You really should sue the fiendish maker of this device. It ran through all of its diagnostic tests flawlessly."

"What will I do now?" lamented John. "It's like she's lost all volition; she's a broken woman."

Patty lay there. Her thoughts were a jumble. *Who are these people near me? Don't they see that I just want to be left alone?* Something nagged at the edges of her consciousness. *Wasn't there something I was supposed to be doing? No, I don't think so. It's so blissful not having anything to do. This is just heavenly."*

"Just look at her," wailed John. "She's lost all will. What will become of us now?"

Patty had complete control.
She'd fix her husband's ills.
He will sustain
Despite the pain
Because it's what she wills.

33 LEAVING NO STONE UNTURNED

Diane sat brooding at her desk. Detective Magnini had called her and told her that they had yet to receive the logs containing Luci's and Sam's emails and security accesses.

Luci had just left for a meeting with the military at Edwards Air Force Base. They were interested in how they could use Coach with their flight and rocket researchers, as well as their test pilots. Diane figured that this was her only chance to get to Ian while he was alone. She hadn't trusted sending an email to him or calling him, since she was sure that Luci was monitoring all communications. Likewise, she couldn't just walk over to his office without Luci spying her.

Now was probably her only chance. She got up and went downstairs to the server room. Ian was always tinkering with the servers, adding disk drives and CPUs in order to improve their performance. Sure enough, she shortly spotted him deep in the innards of one of the cabinets.

"Ian, I need to talk to you about an important matter. Can we go up to your office?"

"Sure, Diane. I was just finishing here. Just let me plug this final cable in. There. OK, let's go."

As they walked back upstairs, Ian asked, "So, what's this all about? You could have sent me an email, you know."

"No, this requires us to talk face to face. This is too important to leave to an email. Plus, I don't want a record of our conversation around that Luci can dig up. It's about her."

Ian blanched. He really didn't want to talk about Luci with anyone. He had been getting more nervous recently that his whole sordid affair with her was going to get out, and then there would be hell to pay. But, as they got to his office, he offered Diane a chair and then sat behind his desk. "So, I'm guessing you were waiting for Luci to be out of the office before we talked? I think that was pretty wise of you. Luci seems to know everything that's going on around here."

"Yes, I'm here exactly for that reason. The police detectives are trying to follow up on Sam's death. The case is still open. I didn't tell you this, but Sam had left me a note the night that he died. He said that Luci was not to be trusted, as she wasn't what she seemed. I know you didn't trust her at first either, but you've been silent the whole time since Sam's death. Since Luci might be involved, you have to help out. Did you know that Sam didn't trust her? Has she done or said anything since Sam died that's suspicious?"

Ian thought for a minute about whether he should say anything. Maybe he could just let this all slide. After all, he really did enjoy the sex and his new Dodge Viper. "Why does it matter? Sam's dead, Luci's in charge, and we are making money hand over fist. Why rock the boat, Diane?"

"Because, this is just insane! Don't you see what Luci is doing? It's immoral, what she's done with Coach. And, I'm starting to believe it's unholy too. Didn't you see her debate with Pastor Isaac on TV? Our seven profiles match the seven deadly sins. That can't be by coincidence. She's up to something evil!"

"Whoa, cool your jets, Diane. I don't believe in that stuff. But, she can be a little devil sometimes," he said and grinned as he thought about some of their sex encounters.

"But Ian, if she's involved, what if one of us is next?"

Ian hadn't thought about that, and didn't like the idea one bit. It would be easy for Luci to do him in during one of their sex sessions. She had become more demanding and domineering with each encounter, and Ian had no willpower when it came to her demands. Yes, if she decided Ian was out, he wasn't going to be able to stop her. She could just tie him up and choke him to death in one of her sex games, or possibly do something worse. Maybe he really should do something now while he still had the chance.

"Well, what I tell you now CANNOT get back to Luci. She can be pretty scary. I swear that sometimes it seems like she's got horns growing out the top of her head."

Diane saw a chance here. "Absolutely. Anything you tell me is in the strictest confidence. I don't want her coming after me either."

"Well, she did happen to order me to delete all of her past emails and system accesses."

"WHAT? And you did that? Oh, Ian, how could you? That's exactly what she would ask if she was guilty!"

"Give me some credit, Diane. I had to obey her. I deleted it all. But, you know, she never said I couldn't make a backup."

Diane jumped up, reached across the desk, hugged Ian and gave him a kiss on the cheek. "Ian, you wonderful man! Quick, give it to me so that I can get it to the detectives."

Ian turned red, rubbed his cheek and then opened one of his desk drawers. "I keep it here on this USB drive. I couldn't keep it online anywhere in case Luci went searching for any traces of it. Whatever you do, you can't let anyone know where you got this. Please promise me."

"I promise. No one will know where I got this. I'll let you know what we find out."

Diane ran back to her office, grabbed her coat and purse and ran out the office to her car, dialing Detective Magnini on her smart phone as she ran. "Tony," she huffed as she got to her car and the police detective picked up. "I'm on my way with the evidence you requested. I'll be there in 15 minutes. Be ready."

34 OUT ON A LIMB

Ghalib and his partner Jasar knocked on the apartment door. "Remember," said Ghalib. "We do not know who this Ajmal is, so we need to exercise extreme caution. It is very mysterious that he acquired both of our names, and it would be most unfortunate if our al-Qaeda cell was discovered before we had a chance to complete our next mission. But perhaps Allah will smile upon us and provide us with another operative in our ongoing battle with 'The Great Satan.'

Just then the door opened. "Greetings," said Ajmal. You must be Ghalib and Jasar. You are the last to arrive. Please come in and sit down. Would you care for a smoke?"

Ghalib looked around as he entered. There were three other Arab-looking men sitting on chairs around the table, smoking hookah pipes. *Well, at least he knows how to treat his guests properly,* he thought. "Yes, that would be most enjoyable."

Ajmal could hardly contain his excitement as he brought over two more pipes. "I am so glad you could all come. I know my invitation was slightly mysterious, but I need some assistance from like-minded individuals."

Jasar interrupted. "Yes, it was most surprising. I, for one, have an unlisted phone number and have only moved here recently. How did you find me?"

"Let me start with why I arranged this meeting. Until recently, I worked at the local GM plant. I worked there for the last two years, and then, out of all the people there, I was the one singled out to lose his job. They told me they had to cut back, but I know it was because of my Pakistani heritage. I will be honest with you all. I am seeking revenge and want to learn how to make a bomb."

One of the guests looked alarmed. "You want to blow people up? That's terrible. I really want no part of that."

"No, no," said Ajmal. "I don't want to hurt anyone. I want to blow up some of the equipment at the plant. I think that would be equal justice for the insult they have caused me. After my years of service, I was treated like the sole of a shoe."

"Well, then, what makes you think any of us can help you?" said Ghalib.

"I have this device here," Ajmal said as he held up his Coach. "It is quite an astonishing piece of technology. You simply ask it for whatever you wish, and it instantly responds with excellently relevant answers. It is like a modern day 'Aladdin's Lamp'! I asked it for people who know how to make bombs, and it found all of you in a few seconds!"

"I can see why it had you contact me," said the guest who had spoken up earlier. "But I just make homemade fireworks for my children. I do not think I can really help you, nor do I want to be part of anything unlawful, for my children's sake. I understand why you might seek revenge, as I'm sure we have all here been subject to discrimination at some time. You have been most gracious, and so I will not say anything to the authorities. Please be careful and do not hurt anyone. Allah be with you." With that, the guest got up and walked out the door.

"If anyone else is uncomfortable with this, please feel free to leave. I will not be insulted," Ajmal said to his remaining guests. The other guests nodded, and then two more left, leaving just Ghalib and Jasar.

"May I see this 'Aladdin's Lamp?'" asked Ghalib. Ajmal gave him his Coach and showed him a log of his requests and Coach's replies.

"This is most astounding! Is this an American military application?"

"No, it should be standard on your device. Perhaps you have not used it enough yet for it to personalize its recommendations."

"I can see that I will need to spend more time learning the intricacies of my device. I am surprised the military has not appropriated it. I myself would find it useful."

"Why? What line of work are you in?"

"Executive recruitment," said Ghalib quickly. "I think I will need to spend more time customizing my device when I leave. Yes, it will be most helpful. For that, I thank you."

"So, neither of you left after I told you my goal. Does that mean you can help me make a bomb?"

Ghalib and Jasar glanced at each other, and Jasar spoke up. "I have a better idea. I make munitions for the military and can make the bomb for you. I suggest three bombs with timers. You want to be able to get away, of course. They will be small and only big enough to disable a large piece of equipment. Since I, um, have a few ready to deliver downstairs in my car, I can go prepare them now and bring them right up. Will that suffice?"

"Oh, Allah has answered my dreams. This is most wonderful. You have given me the opportunity to regain my honor."

Ghalib and Jasar said their goodbyes and left. On the way back to their car, Ghalib said, "That was well done. You will, of course, make sure that the combined strength of the three explosives will do tremendous damage?"

"Absolutely. The fool will not realize how powerful the explosives are and that he might possibly bring the whole plant down upon his head. I will have him tie them all together under the guise of synchronizing the timers, which has no meaning since the mechanism will be taken from a suicide vest. We will have made another blow against the Americans without exposing ourselves. I made sure to steal his Coach device when his back was turned so that we cannot be tracked."

"Most excellent. I will wait in the car while you deliver the explosives back upstairs. Allahu Akbar."

"Allahu Akbar."

Ajmal hunched over the three devices he had placed together under the middle of the automobile assembly line. It was Sunday afternoon; the robots were immobile with a few partially assembled cars sitting on the conveyor belt. He had snuck into the plant using his old access card. They hadn't even bothered to delete his id from their system yet, as if he didn't matter anymore. Just the thought that they had forgotten him already fueled his resolve even more.

Let's see. Jasar said to place all three devices next to each other and to plug the red wires all together, and that would cause the timers on all three to synchronize. OK, here goes.

He attached the wires, and then pushed the center button on the small console. The LEDs on the tiny window lit up. ENTER TIME. Now he had to push the up button for every minute delay that he wanted. *This is going to be great. Three bombs. It's like three wishes from 'Aladdin's Lamp', and I know what to do with the third one. I'm going to put it under my old boss' desk. Won't he be surprised when he comes in tomorrow with all of his papers blown to hell.*

Ajmal pushed the up button ten times and the timer now read 10:00. Jasar's instructions to him were that he should then push the red button on top of a small handheld tube. That would synch the timers and start the countdown, and then he could unplug everything and place the devices in multiple locations.

OK. One bomb for the auto assembly line robots, one for the car parts warehouse, and one for Larry's desk. Here goes. He pushed the red button.

KA-BLAM.

Ajmal felt himself hurled through the air. Parts of the robot line were flying all around him. One of the chains wrapped around his left leg, and another chain wrapped around his right arm. He came to rest hanging upside down from the rafters. He could look up through a gaping hole in the ceiling.

He was in agony. The chain around his leg was up over a rafter, with the other side attached to a large robot arm wedged in the I-beams. Pulling down on the chain attached to his arm was a partially assembled GMC Sierra Denali that had been left on the line.

Well, maybe this wasn't such a good idea after all, he thought, as the weight of the car pulled and pulled until it literally tore him limb from limb.

Ajmal Taqi had a trade,
But then he lost his wage.
He'll get a bomb
To serve Islam
And satisfy his rage.

35 THE SENSIBLE SWAMI

The altercations between Raj and Chandra were becoming more frequent and more heated. Raj tried his best to forgive Chandra for letting a not-so-smartphone bring them both to financial ruin. Acting on Chandra's request, he had actually obtained a second job teaching nights at a local college. Truth was, however, he resented the fact that he had to carry two jobs while Chandra enjoyed her soft life, refusing to get a job and refusing to downsize.

Chandra was angry at Raj for being upset with her. After all, didn't he utter his vows before a priest and promise to care for her? So why the angst?

Raj came home late from his teaching job. He opened the door, walked past Chandra who was busy watching Anderson Cooper on CNN. He entered the bedroom and slammed the door. Chandra followed him in. "Are you still carrying on, Raj? Can't we enjoy our beautiful home together and not have these arguments?"

Raj started to undress for bed. "You know, Chandra, I'm doing my best to keep us afloat. It's a one-sided relationship, though. I give and give and give while you take and take. It's not fair. Unless our circumstances change soon, we may have to consider a divorce. In truth, a number of my female students are interested in me and find me attractive. I've resisted temptation so far, but I don't think I can for much longer. Things have to change."

Chandra was aghast. "Should we see a marriage counselor? What should we do?"

Raj thought for a few moments. "You know, you keep going back to our marriage vows as ammunition for your arguments. Instead, why don't you go see this guy who spoke at one of our company outings?" Raj handed Chandra a business card. "Here. Deepak Bhat is a swami, a mystic and a wise man. Please call him tomorrow and discuss our marriage vows with him in the context of our circumstances. He's quite knowledgeable and, if you present the facts truthfully, I'll abide by his advice. Does that sound fair?"

Chandra tried to force a smile. "Sure. I'll give Deepak a try, but I'm sure he'll support the way I feel."

Chandra and Raj retired to bed, each wide-awake and staring at the ceiling. *Where had love gone? Or was it ever there?"*

Deepak Bhat looked the part of a swami. He was a middle-aged man with a ragged handlebar mustache. He was wearing a white turban as he greeted Chandra at the door. "Good afternoon, Chandra. I'm glad to meet you. Please come in and sit down."

They greeted each other with the traditional Pranamasana and then sat opposite each other in the living room. Deepak started the dialogue. "So, Chandra, I understand that you have some marital difficulties. Please explain them as best you can, then I'll see how I can help you."

Chandra grimaced. "This isn't easy for me, but I'll do the best I can.

My husband Raj and I were married in India before a priest. We had a traditional wedding with Raj saying the eight ceremonial vows."

"Yes, Chandra, I know them well."

"We settled in a beautiful home and were quite comfortable until we made some bad investments and lost a great deal of our money. That's when the trouble started."

"So tell me. What were your discussions about after all of

this happened?"

"Raj wanted me to give up my beautiful home and downsize. He wanted me to seek employment. I told him that doing this would violate his sacred vows and that he should take a second job until we could make ends meet."

Deepak mused. "Hmm. Let's look at each vow, one by one.

Does he consider you 'the better half?'"

"Yes, I think so, at least some of the time."

"Are you in charge of the home? Do you plan things together with him?"

"Well, that's a problem. If I'm in charge of the home, he cannot insist that we downsize, right?"

"I'll save my comments for later, Chandra. Does he treat your shortcomings with understanding?"

"Not lately. He's been pretty angry about everything."

"I see. Has he looked at other women?"

"Just recently. He says he's been faithful, however."

"This is serious, Chandra. No wonder you came here today. Does he treat you as a friend?"

"He used to. There is too much anger now. We're always fighting."

"This is bad. Do you argue in front of others?"

"Oh, no. Not at all."

"Hmm. Is he courteous? Do you compromise?"

"He used to be courteous. Not any more. We seem totally unable to reach a compromise on our finances though."

"Finally, Chandra, do you think he would care for you even if you behaved wrongly?"

"I think not, Deepak. He has just started discussions about separation and divorce."

"An important question, Chandra. Do you love him?"

"I think so. Our marriage was arranged and I'm not sure I know what love is. We had a comfortable life together. That's love, is it not?"

Deepak thought to himself. *This is one lost soul. She's not in love at all. She just wants to be cared for. In fact, she never spoke the word "love." Perhaps I should start with teaching her the concept of being in a partnership.* "Here's what I think, Chandra. You have real trouble and you need to sit and talk lovingly. You need to start the conversations by expressing your love, then get into problem solving together. Marriage is a partnership, correct?'

"Yes, it should be."

"Good. Then you know what to do. There is neither 'right' nor 'wrong' here. It's about lovingly solving problems together. I have a small activity to help you take those first steps towards becoming a true partner with your husband. Come with me."

"Thank you, Deepak. You really are a swami and most wise." Chandra smiled. She thought it was good how Deepak agreed with everything she had said so far. She could not wait to go home and face Raj. Then she had an awful thought. "Hey, Deepak. If you're really a swami, do you have a pet cobra? This activity doesn't involve one, does it?"

Deepak laughed. "Not all swamis have cobras, but I actually do have one in the basement. Do not worry. Come with me."

Chandra followed Deepak downstairs. In the middle of his dimly lit basement was a large glass enclosure with an enormous king cobra asleep in the bottom of the cage. "How exciting! What do I do now?"

"Stand here on this piece of tape that is a few feet from the cage. Now, I will sit next to you and start playing music on my pungi. I want you to start swaying left and right to the music. Watch the snake. Soon he will rise from the bottom of his cage and do the same. Match your swaying to the snake's. You and the snake will be partners in a dance."

Swami Deepak started to play, and Chandra started swaying. After ten seconds, Chandra wailed, "This is boring! Nothing's happening! How long do I have to do this for?"

"Patience, child. A partnership requires patience."

Chandra swayed left and right for another ten seconds. "I'm tired. This is too hard."

"Diligence, child. A partnership requires diligence," Swami Deepak calmly explained and continued to play the snake charming music.

Chandra swayed two more times. "He's not paying attention to me! Pay attention, snake!"

"Temperance, child. A partnership requires..."

Unfortunately for Chandra, temperance, or self-restraint, was not one of her strong suits. She ran over and banged on the glass of the cobra's cage to get its attention.

"NO! TEMPERANCE!" screamed the swami, struggling to rise.

The cobra sprung quickly into action, flying from the bottom of the cage and biting Chandra on the cheek. And that was all that Chandra would ever remember.

Chandra Chopra had a match
Which she would soon betroth.
She'll lounge around,
A princess crowned
And live a life of sloth.

36 EXPOSED

Diane arrived at the precinct, parked her car and hustled inside. Tony and Jim were waiting for her. "Let's go into a conference room where we can have some privacy," Tony said. "There is also a computer with Internet access there that we can use. Do you have the thumb drive with you?"

"Yes, here it is," Diane said, handing it to him as they walked into the room. Jim closed the door as Tony and Diane pulled up chairs by the computer, and then Jim went to stand behind them to watch.

Tony inserted the drive into a USB slot on the side, and then selected to look at the file folders with Windows Explorer from the pop-up menu. There were three file folders listed: emails, login-logout-times and security-system-accesses.

Tony opened the emails file first. It showed 5,483 emails. "Ugh," said Tony. "Where do we start?"

"Try clicking on the tab at the top to sort the files by sender," said Jim. "Let's see who's been emailing her. Diane, you know which email ids are from ECS employees, so just point out to us ones you don't recognize."

As Tony paged down past the id's starting with 'A', Diane spotted a strange one. "Stop. Open up that one by Brother Bernard." Tony double-clicked on the file to open it.

"My Dear Sister Ferguson,

Thank you for attending our private session last night and providing us with incisive information on how to summon major demons. Your demonstration was most convincing. As you know, our rites were sorely lacking in this regard, and we had only been able to summon what seemed to be one imp on all of our previous attempts. Our rites have now taken on a whole new dimension.

You are welcome to come to a sacrifice in your honor next week. Please call me to provide the most auspicious times for us to provide such a ritual.

Yours in eternity,
Brother Bernard."

Upon reading this, Tony reflexively fingered his Sir Galahad medallion that his wife gave him when he joined the force and that he kept under his shirt.

Diane crossed herself.

"You've got to be kidding me," Jim said with a wry grin. "People still believe in that shit? What is this, the Middle Ages?"

Diane turned around to look at him. "You shouldn't be so snarky. Some famous people believed in the occult and black magic, going all the way back to Sir Isaac Newton. If you want a more recent case, Jack Parson, the inventor of solid rocket fuel, always prayed to demons before a test launch. He also attended black magic rites and orgies. The government canned him after the FBI discovered his doings. He eventually blew himself up in the 1950s in his home lab. Rumors were that it happened while he was summoning demons. Perhaps he succeeded."

Jim rolled his eyes. "OK, fine. So she believes this stuff too. That won't get her arrested. Let's keep looking."

Tony paged further down the email list. "Stop," said Diane, pointing at one of the items. "Open that one from Lee Woo Yeun. That looks like a Korean name and email address. We never could find out anything of Luci's past. Perhaps this will tell us something.

Tony opened it, and they all quickly read the note. It was a confirmation that PSY had been contacted and paid to create a music video about Coach and the new slogan, as per Luci's request. The email also stated that Luci should not contact Lee Woo any further, as the uproar in South Korea over her online impersonations and subsequent accidental death of a child had finally settled down. The end of the note had his address and business phone number, something than many people automatically attach at the bottom of their corporate communications.

"Wow, that's some bad mojo there," said Jim. "Let's call him up and ask a few questions. It's late in Korea right now, but maybe he's still working."

Tony dialed the international number, and after a few rings it was picked up. "Is this Mr. Lee Woo Yeun? This is Detective Magnini from the United States calling on an urgent matter. I have two others here on the line," said Tony as he put the call on speaker.

"Why yes, it is, Detective Magnini. I was just about to leave for home. What can I help you with?"

"We are investigating a Ms. Luci Ferguson on a suspicious death here in California, and we came across your name. Can you tell us a bit more about her? I understand that she was involved in another suspicious death there in South Korea."

Lee Woo quickly outlined what had happened and how Luci had impersonated a child called Elsie, which resulted in a Korean couple feeding her online child avatar and neglecting their own real handicapped child, causing their child to starve to death. He continued, "If you want my advice, be rid of her as quickly as possible. The police here could do nothing due to her political connections. She is still a secret member of our board, but, as you might imagine, we try to communicate with her as little as possible."

"Thank you, Mr. Lee. Is there anything else you could tell us?" said Tony.

"Yes, I suggest you look at the times of her off-hour home accesses and security logs, and try to equate the times of them to suspicious happenings. That is how we discovered her off-hours activities as the Elsie avatar."

"Thank you for your time," said Tony as he hung up. "Well, Luci certainly seems to have participated in at least one death overseas, but that's not enough proof to arrest her."

"Right," said Jim. "Let's look at her home login activity next.

Tony opened up the login-logout-times file. It had three columns: Date, Login, Logout. They quickly scanned the list.

"Wait," said Jim. "I know that date and time. That's the day we went to investigate that huge guy who choked to death. And look at the time that Luci was online – she logged in at 10:45 pm and logged out at 11:23 pm. The lab guys told me that the SIM analysis showed that the guy's smartphone reloaded itself at 11:23. That's mighty suspicious that the times match. And the coroner said that he died somewhere between 11:15 and 11:45 that night."

"Good work, Jim," said Tony.

"Perfect. Let's go arrest her," said Diane. "She's evil and this proves it."

"Hold on, Diane," said Tony. "This is circumstantial evidence. It doesn't prove she was directly involved. We need something else first. Let's look at the security system accesses."

Tony opened the third of the three files. There were only

a few entries.

"Wait! Look! I recognize that one," said Diane. That's Sam's smartphone number. And it says next to it 'STOLEN' with a time of 7:13pm. I think that's the date he died too in the last column."

"You're right," said Tony. "I do recognize that date as the date of his death. And the time is about right from the coroner's report."

"Maybe he thought his phone was stolen and reported it just before he died?" said Jim.

"No," said Diane. "These are Luci's security accesses. It means that SHE put it into the system then. And look here. It says REACTIVATE at 7:45 pm."

"What does the system do with those commands?" asked Tony.

"The 'stolen' command would have shut Sam's smartphone down completely. He would not have been able to make any phone calls for help. And, once reactivated, anyone analyzing his smartphone would not have noticed anything suspicious."

"That's good enough for me," said Jim. "This should be enough for us to get a warrant for her arrest. Let's go get her."

"Wait," said Diane. "She's into the occult, sacrifices and demonology. Who knows what kinds of traps she might have in her house. You can't just go marching into her lair. I suggest we call my pastor for advice before we go. He has experience with these types of situations."

"Tony, are you going to listen to this?" said Jim. "Are we going to carry bibles and hang crosses around our necks too to protect us before we go?"

"Hey, watch it, Jim. Have some respect," said Tony. "It wouldn't hurt to get some extra advice on this one. Let's call in to get the warrant. While we wait for it to come through, Diane, you call your pastor and put him on speaker phone so we can hear what he thinks."

37 THE FACTS, JUST THE FACTS

While at police headquarters, Diane called Pastor Ted Johnson. Pastor Ted's secretary answered her call and patched Diane over to the pastor. An anxious Diane started the conversation. "I'm sure glad you were available, Pastor Ted. I'm here at the San Francisco Precinct with Detectives Tony Magnini and Jim Kirkland. Do you have some time to talk?"

Pastor Ted responded. "Sure, Diane. I was going to head out to meet with Pastor Joseph, but that can wait. This sounds urgent. Are you in trouble?"

"No, Ted. But the many sins of my employer, Luci Ferguson, are finally coming home to roost. I think we were right about her, and she seems to be in a great deal of trouble. May I put you on speaker?"

"Yes, Diane. This should be a most interesting conversation!"

"Thanks... I'll start with what I know and then the detectives can jump in. First off, we know that Luci was involved in demonology. We have conclusive proof of this in one of her emails. What's more disconcerting, however, is that there seems to be solid evidence that she was actively involved in at least two deaths."

"I'm not surprised at this, Diane. Please give me some of the details."

"This is Detective Magnini, Pastor Ted. The first case is that of Mr. Billy Wilson. Detective Kirkland and I were actually involved in this case. Mr. Wilson was an obese gentleman who seemed to die choking on his dinner of scallops, frogs' legs and cherry pie."

"So why does this implicate Ms. Ferguson?"

"She was on the phone with Mr. Wilson immediately before his death, and yet she never reported anything. Let me go on to the second case, that of Mr. Sam Washburn, the former CEO of ECS."

"What? She might have been involved there also?"

"It seems so, Pastor Ted. She shut down his smartphone at the exact time of his death."

"Was she there at the scene of the death?"

"No. She did it remotely. He was unable to call for help after his 'accident.' There's actually one more case. It seems that she was instrumental in the death of a South Korean infant. We learned this from a conversation with her former employer in South Korea."

Pastor Ted paused for a moment. "She's an evil person, for sure. But is all of this sufficient evidence to arrest her? Tell me again how Mr. Washburn died."

"He burned to death in his fire pit after it leaked oil."

Pastor Ted paused once more. "Hmm…and the other fellow choked on frog's legs. Let me think. Hold on…"

Pastor Ted put the phone on hold, and then returned in a few minutes. "Thanks for waiting. I had to pray to the Lord for guidance. If Ms. Ferguson is who I suspect she is, we're all going to need some divine guidance. I have a hunch, a wild hunch. Watch for my email to Diane in a few minutes. I am going over to the other room to send something, and then I'll be right back."

Tony replied "You got it Pastor; we'll hold on. Thanks for your help!"

Jim could not resist commenting. "This is crazy. What's

he possibly going to send that could be of any help? He's not a cop. This is all mumbo-jumbo."

Diane smiled. "No he is not a cop, but watch now for the power of prayer!"

Two minutes later, Diane read her pastor's email aloud. "Here it is. The subject is 'The Seven Deadly Sins and Their Punishments.' Here is a list:

'1. Pride= Broken on a wheel.
2. Anger= Dismembered alive.
3. Envy= Put in freezing water.
4. Sloth= Thrown into snake pits.
5. Gluttony= Force-fed rats, toads and snakes.
6. Lust= Smothered against fire and brimstone.
7. Greed= Boiled in oil.'"

Jim laughed again. "What the hell does he mean by this?"

Tony, however, turned white. "Jesus, Mary and Joseph! I get it. Billy choked on frogs' legs. Frogs as a punishment for gluttony. Makes perfect sense."

Jim mused. "OK, but it's a stretch. What about Mr. Washburn? How do you tie his death to that list?"

Diane responded to Jim. "He died in a fire."

"Yes, but it was an oil fire in his fire pit." said Tony. "The oil in his fire pit leaked and he was literally boiled in oil!"

Diane thought for a second. "But Sam was not greedy. At least I didn't think so."

Tony thought for a moment also. "It doesn't matter what you thought of Washburn. It matters what Ferguson thought of him! You know what? Pastor Ted, you may have found something. Diane, let me and Jim work on this for a while."

Tony handed Diane his business card with contact information. "Here's my email address. Please forward your pastor's email to me right now, then Jim and I will try to search the national database for recent deaths, cross-correlating them to the seven punishments. It's worth a shot anyway. It may just add to our case for a warrant. Head on home, and we'll let you and the pastor know what we find. Thank you both for your help."

Diane thought a moment. "OK, that sounds good. Thank you, Pastor Ted."

"Be careful child," said Pastor Ted before he hung up. "Ms. Ferguson is still at large. Pray fervently until this is resolved."

The next day, Detectives Tony and Jim conducted a systematic search within the national database for deaths within the past two years. They quickly concluded that looking for "broken on a wheel" would be difficult, as there were thousands of car accidents. The next punishment was "dismembered"; when they searched on that term they found the police report on Ajmal Taqi, where it stated that he was irate, having been fired by his employer and seeking revenge. Good. One down.

When they searched for "freezing water," they found nothing of significance. When they searched for "snake," they had three hits. Two of the hits related to snakes biting animal trainers, but the third was the one showing that Chandra Razdan died of snakebite in the home of Mr. Bhat. After several phone calls and a conversation with the swami, they concluded that Chandra was, in fact, quite lazy. Two down, and this was getting interesting…

They searched for the word "smothered" and located six

police reports. Five were not of any interest, but the sixth report was the one about Eric Kruger, a convicted pedophile. Three down and enough information to go to the next level. They called Diane at home leaving a message that she should look up the records of Ajmal, Chandra, and Eric.

The next day, Diane returned their call saying that they all were owners of the Coach device.

Armed with the times of death, the detectives again accessed the ECS security file. Sure enough, the file indicated that, in Eric's case, Ms. Ferguson had provided a security pass-through to ECS partners, thus abetting Eric's crime. They had enough evidence to secure an arrest warrant.

Tony and Jim left another message at Diane's home bringing her up to date and suggesting that they pick up Diane, go to Pastor Ted's house and then on to the Ferguson residence for an arrest. The wheels were finally in motion and Diane would signal the go-ahead date and time.

.

38 JOHNNY, GET YOUR GUN

Johnny Esposito's fantasies were becoming more and more a reality, clouding his already troubled life. He was in an empty shell of a marriage and still clinging on to the hope that he and his neighbor Debbie might hookup for a weekend tryst. His love life with wife Joan was nil, he found himself barely able to "go through the marital motions."

His major obstacle was Raul Arroyo, his neighbor Debbie's husband. If he could be exactly like Raul and then did away with him, he could snuggle up to Debbie while offering his most sincere condolences. Passionate sex would follow and they would both live happily ever after. And, he would have all of Raul's stuff too. He would have his house, his car AND his wife. How was he to track down Raul and get rid of him? He'd need the perfect time and place. He would need to mimic Raul as much as possible.

Johnny asked his Coach 5.0 how best to track his neighbor. He was already "friends" with Debbie and Raul on Facebook, peering constantly into their lives. Coach replied that it could use that information to get even more intelligence on his neighbors' spending habits and whereabouts at all times. Johnny gave Coach their Facebook IDs and told it to start. Then, to fuel his fantasy further, he purchased the sultry voice of Ertha Kitt. Now wouldn't that be a hoot to get all of his future advice in that voice?

Johnny had a fantasy;
He craved his neighbor's wife.

###

Johnny loved his Coach. Ertha Kitt was continually providing him with daily reminders and sage advice. He could easily track any of his "friends," especially Raul and Debbie.

Coach had taken the information Johnny had provided and searched for email IDs matching the neighbors' names on all the major vendors: AOL, Gmail, Comcast, and Verizon. It then tried the most common passwords that people used, such as 'password', '123456' and 'abc123'. Coach was patient. It only tried a few passwords a day, so that the email providers would issue no warnings.

Coach finally got a hit for Debbie Arroyo at aol.com with the 21st most used password of 'jesus'. Once in, it then tried the various online credit card systems for the same ID. The passwords were different, but it was a simple matter to invoke the 'Forgot password' function on them, which naturally sent a temporary password back to Debbie's AOL id to allow access, and thus giving Coach access to their credit card information.

Soon, Johnny knew every purchase that the Arroyo's made. He was getting tired of Eartha Kitt, but found that, since his mother also had Coach, he could have Coach deliver its advice in his mother's voice.

Soon, Coach started telling him what to buy. Johnny started buying the exact same items as his neighbors. He was going to make it so easy for Debbie to accept him in their new lives. As the pressure built to buy more and more, with Coach telling him how he could be a better man, he started to call his Coach 'Mother.'

"But first, you need to clear the air with Joan," 'Mother' told him. "You owe it to your wife to tell her it's not working."

'Yes, Mother," he told his Coach. "I'm just not in love with her anymore. We've been married for nine years, but it seems like an eternity. She must know that I'm unhappy. God knows, she's miserable too. We'll both be better off. Yes, we'll both be better off."

Johnny had a fantasy;

He craved his neighbor's wife.
They'll go away

Both of the Esposito's children were sleeping over at their friends' homes. Johnny was watching a movie on TV that Saturday night. Joan had finished cleaning up the dinner dishes when she walked into the living room. "I think I'll go lie down for a while," said Joan. "You seem to be into your movie anyway."

"Are you happy?" asked Johnny. "We are ships passing in the night. There's nothing left in our marriage."

"How can you say that?" stammered Joan. "I have a headache and want to lie down and you turn that into a marital crisis? What the hell is going on? And what's all this junk you keep buying? We can't afford any of it!"

"Sit down, Joan. Let's be realistic about our issues. We never have sex anymore. We have no intimacy. We do our daily routines and put up a good front to our friends and neighbors, but what do we really have? When is the last time you said you loved me?"

"Well, asshole, When is the last time you said you loved me? It's not all about me, you know! Are you fucking someone else?"

"No! I've never been unfaithful. I just have no feelings for you. I haven't felt any attachment for years. You have to feel the same way..."

"You have too much time on your hands, John. I go to work, run the house, take care of the kids and do the shopping. I don't have time to dwell on my feelings. I just keep going...." Joan burst into tears.

"Let's try to remain friends, Joan. I really think we

should talk about a separation."

Joan walked into the bedroom and slammed the door.

Johnny pulled out his Coach and talked to it. "It went well, Mother. Soon I'll be free."

Johnny had a fantasy;
He craved his neighbor's wife.
They'll go away
To play all day

It was late November. Joan had moved into her parents' home with the kids while Johnny was tracking Raul's every move on his Coach. Mother had been telling him every new purchase that Raul had made. Johnny was ordering the same things in order to be exactly like him for when Debbie and he were together. Recently, he had found that Raul liked to hunt, and Mother had purchased for him a fine high-powered hunting rifle. Mother had also purchased for him a new camouflage outfit and very large hiking boots.

Finally, the opportunity came. Raul said on Facebook that he was going on a deer hunting trip with his buddies. Brant Lake, New York. Yes, a hunting accident would be perfect. The deer-hunting season was coming up in two weeks, so he had time to ask Mother to book a hotel room and ask for time off from work. Johnny had never shot a rifle before, but Mother told him it was a simple matter to look through the scope, center the crosshairs, and then shoot. Yes, the time was here. Mother was preparing him perfectly to take Raul's place at Debbie's side.

Brant Lake would normally be about a five-hour drive from Port Jefferson Station. With the snow on the ground, however, it took Johnny more like seven hours to get there.

The new boots that Mother had bought him felt strange and uncomfortable on his feet as he drove, but he figured that they would break in shortly. He checked into his room at the Tumble Inn B&B, about fifteen miles from the hunting area. The next morning at 3:00 AM, Johnny put on his red hunting jacket, grabbed his gun and Mother and headed out to wherever the GPS tracking would take him. Johnny's mouth was dry with anticipation as he headed out in his car.

After a slow, arduous drive in the snow and ice, Johnny arrived a few hundred yards from Raul's hunting lodge. He parked his car and trekked through the snow, being guided carefully by Mother. "Be careful, Johnny. One foot in front of the other. Don't step on any twigs. Step in the nice soft squishy mud to muffle your footsteps," she stated. Just before dawn, he heard several men's voices. He crouched down and listened carefully. Yes, it was Raul. *Here we go, Raul. Say goodbye to your friends. Say goodbye to Debbie. She'll be all mine tomorrow.*

Johnny spotted Raul next to a large tulip tree. Raul was crouching down in anticipation of taking a shot. Johnny hoped to get his shot off at the same time Raul fired. He had to be very careful.

A five-point deer came into view at perhaps a hundred yards from Raul. Johnny crouched down and aimed his rifle at Raul. He looked through the viewfinder, as Mother instructed him to. Sure enough, the scope's crosshairs were perfectly centered on Raul's head.

Raul fired at the deer and missed. Johnny fired at Raul but also just missed, his bullet slamming into the bark of the tulip tree above Raul's head.

Johnny, being a real novice when it came to guns, had never read anything about them, relying totally on his Coach device. It had never provided the information that you needed to first adjust your targeting scope to ensure accuracy on any new rifle.

"What the fuck!" yelled Raul. He got on his feet and stormed towards Johnny. Johnny ran as fast as he could, but the large boots were killing his feet, and the snow and ice hampered his progress. Shit! I have to get away! I can't let him see me here!

Johnny saw a nearby embankment. He'd hide in the bushes next to the embankment.

Johnny dropped his rifle and jumped towards the nearby embankment. As he landed, his boot soles slipped; they were covered in that soft squishy mud Mother had told him to use to silence his steps. He tumbled head over heels and past the potential hiding spot in the underbrush. He tumbled over the edge of the embankment and into the cold river below, hitting his head on a boulder as he fell into the awaiting river.

Johnny never felt anything more. The icy water claimed him before he could ever regain consciousness. Mother floated away down the river and then sank into the leviathan depth.

Johnny had a fantasy;
He craved his neighbor's wife.
They'll go away
To play all day
For envy rules his life.

39 TO BE PREPARED IS HALF THE VICTORY

One week later, Diane ascertained that Luci was at home for the evening. She called Detectives Kirkland and Magnini and then drove to Pastor Ted's house while awaiting the squad car.

Tony hung up the phone, and opened his desk drawer. *This is one of the most mysterious cases I've ever been involved with. Black magic and people dying according to some medieval scripture; who would have ever dreamed this up?* He pulled a box of cartridges out of his drawer labeled Winchester Black Talons. They hadn't made this line in years, partly because of an infamous shooting his precinct had been involved in. The whole idea of these black bullets was to shatter upon hitting something, so as to minimize collateral damage if you missed. However, the follow-up media reports had screamed that, "This bullet kills you better; its six razor-like claws unfold on impact, expanding to nearly three times the bullet's diameter."

The replacement series, the Ranger SXT's, quieted the media, but they all joked here at the precinct that SXT stood for 'Same eXact Thing.' They now used the latest PDX1's, but Tony was nostalgic for these old cartridges. He slowly loaded his gun with the Talons. *I think the black paint-like lubricant coating on these bullets is just what I need for a case involving black magic,* he mused.

"Let's go Jim. Let's get a move on," he yelled towards his partner.

###

When Tony and Jim arrived, Pastor Ted requested they come in for a few moments. The detectives were puzzled but acquiesced. After everyone was seated, Pastor Ted started his cautionary note. "I won't take long, but I wanted to tell all of you that this will not be an ordinary arrest. I suspect Ms. Ferguson has supernatural powers, but I cannot gauge the extent. I have assembled a kit for our visit." Pastor Ted plopped a duffle bag on the table, opening it to reveal that it contained some crosses, vials of what looked like water, a Bible and a can of Morton's salt.

Jim could not contain a brief laugh. "C'mon Pastor. What is this, <u>The Omen</u>? You're not going to stop the arrest and do an exorcism, are you? That's stuff for the movies!"

"You're very naïve, Detective Kirkland," said Pastor Ted impatiently. "You took math courses, right?"

A puzzled Jim responded "Yes, but…"

"OK. Think of the universe as an n-dimensional space. We can only view three dimensions, but there is also the dimension of time and, I believe, an additional spiritual dimension. Angels and demons can ignore time and move easily back and forth from their spiritual dimension into our three-dimensional space. That's how Ms. Ferguson got here and how she will most likely exit. You've heard stories about people on their deathbeds seeing angels? Well, I believe that, as we die, we get an early glimpse into the spiritual dimension."

"Okaaayyy. I never thought of it that way," said a more thoughtful Jim. "You have my undivided attention. Go on…"

"I believe that good and evil are real forces in the spiritual dimension, affecting mortals in our space. In our laws of physics, every action has an opposite and equal reaction. I believe that this is true in the spiritual realm. Good forces are balanced by evil forces. What that means for us is that if we are faced with pure evil, we cannot 'turn the other cheek,' as it were. We must fight back with the powers of goodness and faith."

"I get your drift, Pastor. That's where the exorcism

comes in?"

"Partly. In truth we need to personally trust Christ, the One who has met the enemy head-on and triumphed. That's our one and only hope."

"Fine, Pastor. You can have our backs. I'll rely on my wits and my trusty service revolver, if you don't mind."

Tony could not keep quiet any more. He rubbed his chest, where his 'Sir Galahad' medal lay. "And what about original sin and the Garden of Eden? Where does that fit in with evil forces and multiple dimensions?"

"Good question. I think the Garden of Eden is a metaphor, instead of an actual location in space and time. I believe that some day we will learn that some people are born 'bad' and that evil can be a complex genetic disorder. My kit may work even on a person who is not possessed, if they truly believe that they are. Don't quote me on that, please!"

Diane had been keeping quiet, but she had to interrupt. "All of this reminds me of a quote from Thomas Jefferson. 'Do not bite at the bait of pleasure, till you know there is no hook beneath it.'

Diane continued, "You know, don't you, that our focus has been on Luci, but she's just one-half the problem. Over the past months she's created Coach into an intelligent beast that thinks as she does. Luci already did her work. Coach works very well without her and can continue to wreak havoc on the world. It is the perfect 'bait of pleasure.' Luci is probably limited in her powers, but Coach is not. We need to take care of Luci today but our work is not done until we dismember the ECS servers and their backups."

Everyone knew that Diane was right. They knew that their work was cut out for them as they got into the car and drove to Luci's house.

40 AN EXORCISM IN FUTILITY?

Tony stopped the squad car in front of Luci's house, and they all piled out and stood by her front door as he pounded on the door. "Police! Open up!" he bellowed.

The door slowly opened. There stood Luci, clad in a bright red Japanese kimono with a fire-breathing dragon print on the front. "Well, well. What a congregation. And I see you have a man of the cloth there. Have you come to worship me?" Luci laughed.

"Ms. Luci Ferguson, we have a warrant for your arrest. Please come with us down to the station," said Tony.

"Of course, but I'm sure this is some misunderstanding. As you can see, I'm not quite dressed for the occasion. Please come in. Perhaps we can talk this over," Luci said as she gestured for them to enter.

They all passed through the doorway and into Luci's 'Great Hall.' Jim whistled as he looked around. The huge cathedral ceiling was painted black with the constellations of the zodiac etched upon it. On the walls were hanging paintings that depicted various horrible scenes of people being tortured by demons. He noted that one of them showed victims being force fed toads and snakes. *Oh, you got to be kidding me,* he thought.

Luci kept walking and they followed her into the kitchen. She went over and poured herself a glass of wine from a bottle sitting on the counter. Meanwhile, Pastor Ted hung back, and then ducked away into the hall while Luci's back was turned.

Luci turned around. "So, what is this warrant all about? What am I accused of?"

"Ms. Ferguson, we have evidence that you had shut

down Sam Washburn's smartphone at the time of his death, making it impossible for him to call for help. We also have evidence that you abetted a Mr. Eric Kruger in the sexual exploitation of a minor. We have suspicious evidence of other incidents, but only two are needed for a warrant. Please come quietly."

Suddenly Pastor Ted appeared behind Luci. "Satan, Lucifer, Beelzebub!" he shouted and threw down on the counter a set of black robes, some black candles and a black handled, double-edged Atheme ceremonial dagger. "These are all used in satanic rituals," he yelled. "Be gone, Satan!" he screamed and threw some holy water in Luci's face.

"Gah," shouted Luci and wiped her face with a section of her kimono. "What is WRONG with you?" she said as she stepped forward to confront the pastor.

Pastor Ted backpedaled, and quickly threw a line of salt on the ground. "You shall not pass!" he yelled.

"You poor pathetic fool," growled Luci as she kicked the salt aside, continuing to come forward. "Don't you know that only works on minor demons? If you really think I am Satan, you'll have to do better than that!" she laughed.

Pastor Ted whipped out a large cross and thrust it forward against Luci's forehead. He screamed, "The power of Christ compels you."

Luci let out a hideous howl. "Owww, that HURTS you fucker!"

Diane crossed herself as Luci hopped around with her hands on her face. Tony muttered, "Jesus, Mary and Joseph. I never would have believed it." Jim just stared, stupefied, and said, "My God, I can't believe it really worked!"

Luci stopped hopping, her hands slid down off of her face, and her howl turned to a sneering laugh. "You morons.

The old fool got salt all over that cross, and I have a fresh cut on my hairline from this morning. Of course it hurts! If you mental midgets are finished, then get out of here before I call my lawyer and tell him I'm a victim of police brutality!"

"You can call your lawyer from the precinct, Ms. Ferguson," said Tony. "We have a valid warrant, so you need to come with us."

"Fine. Let me go and change," said Luci as she gathered up her black robe and other items that the pastor had dumped on the counter. "And don't touch any more of my stuff!" she yelled over her shoulder as she stormed off in a huff.

They all walked back into the entryway by the front door. "Pastor, did you see any cuts on her forehead?" Diane asked.

"No, I didn't see anything. I think she was lying," said Pastor Ted.

"Well, she did say it was on her hairline," said Tony, "so you might not have noticed."

Jim was busy looking at more of the horrific paintings, when he saw a form run past one of the windows. "Tony, we've got a runner. Let's go!" he shouted. He opened the door and ran out, followed by his partner. Diane and Pastor Ted looked at each other, and then followed in pursuit.

Jim's Parkour training kicked in. He saw some garbage cans on the ground that Luci had obviously knocked over to slow him down, and he vaulted easily over them. Suddenly, out of an alleyway to his right, three large black Dobermans dashed at him, growling and gnashing their teeth furiously. He jumped high and sideways right at the dogs, and shoulder rolled over the first dog, kicked off the back of the second one, and did another roll over the third. As he landed, he jumped off one wall of the alley, over to the other side, and did a wall climb and a top out onto the roof.

"Watch out, Tony, three hounds from hell," he yelled down at his partner. "You take the low road, and I'll take the high." He sprinted along the rooftop, swung around a pole to change direction, and leaped onto the next roof. In the distance behind him, he heard his partner fire off five shots at the dogs.

At the edge of the fourth roof, Jim stopped and crouched. He tried to slow his breathing. *OK, she's got to come this way any second*, he thought. *She's going to get a taste of what happens when you go up against the mighty Jimbo.* Then he saw her, creeping along trying to be quiet. *Wait for it; wait for it,* he thought.

Just as he was about to drop down, he saw Luci jerk her head and look up at him. Jim jumped. He saw her fling her hand up at him, and something flashed by his face. *What? Ninja stars? REALLY?* He saw her fling her other hand, and Jim contorted in mid-air. The stars missed! But, in the process, he was out of position. He felt his ankle pop as he landed, accompanied by a searing pain.

He tried to get up, but fell back down. *Damn, she's getting away*, he thought. *How did she know I was up there?* He watched as Luci ran around the bend.

At that same moment, Luci was thinking, *I'm pretty sure I can grab a working car over here. If I can do that, I can get away. I have lots of money stashed in various overseas accounts. I'll hire a private jet and fly to Mexico, and from there go to another country and start over. Maybe I'll go back to Asia. They don't have any of these holier than though priests over there.* She spotted the closed gates up ahead.

Seconds later, Tony ran up to his partner, who was on the ground holding his ankle. "Jim, are you OK?"

"Yeah, I'm fine. I was just a tad too slow. She's just up

ahead. Before I jumped down, I saw what looked like an auto recycling center. She must be headed for that. Watch out, she's got sharp objects to throw at you. I almost had her."

"I'll get her. Don't worry," said Tony as he ran ahead. When he rounded the bend, he saw the gates at the entrance to the center almost torn from their hinges. *Man, they never take care of anything at these junkyards,* he thought. He pulled out his revolver and crept ahead.

There, in the glow of the auto recycling center incinerator, he saw her silhouette. "Give it up, Ms. Ferguson. You're cornered. Come quietly before something bad happens."

Luci turned around to face him, her left arm straight out towards him with her palm open and empty. "Be reasonable, Detective. Let me go, and I can make you wildly rich. You can't be making much on a policeman's salary. We could have a great time together, you and I."

"No deal, lady. Just lie on the ground and …"

He saw Luci's other hand reach behind her, and then flick forward, hurling a wicked, black-handled dagger at him. As it hit Tony in the chest, he felt a searing pain and fired one of his Black Talon rounds, hitting Luci. He then fell backwards, banging his head on the pavement.

Pastor Ted arrived huffing on the scene, and saw Luci stagger and trip over a tire iron on the ground, and then fall into the incinerator. Luci let out a final scream as the incinerator burned her to ashes. An ominous black cloud rose up and hovered over her remains.

Pastor Ted fell to his knees, raised both arms to the sky and shouted:

"God arises;

His enemies are scattered
And those who hate Him flee before Him.
As smoke is driven away,
So are they driven;
As wax melts before the fire,
So the wicked perish at the presence of God."

A wind howled around him, and the black cloud was hurled upwards and swirled into oblivion.

Diane arrived and rushed over to check on Tony. She lifted his head onto her lap. "Tony, Tony, are you OK?"

Tony groggily shook his head. "You know, I think I am." He lifted up his shirt, and saw that his gunmetal Galahad shield dog tag that his wife had given him had split in two. "How about that? It looks like it stopped the dagger."

Diane looked down and saw the black-handled Atheme ceremonial dagger. "We shouldn't have let her retrieve this evil thing from the counter with the robes," she said. Diane picked up the dagger and threw it into the incinerator, where it hissed and slowly melted. "You know, we are really lucky that Luci hadn't had a chance to spread her deviltry beyond Eden's servers in the USA. She planned on going global next month."

"So what are you going to do next?" asked Tony.

"I guess since I'm the senior exec, I am now the new CEO. I'm going to go back and make sure everything at the company is dismantled. I'm going to delete Coach and dissolve the company."

Pastor Ted got up from his knees and walked over to them. "She stumbled on iron there at the end. The ancient literature says that iron is inimical to demons. And I think the iron in the incinerator helped. Even so, we cannot rely on purely physical means to end Satan's plans on Earth. As the Bible says, "so put on the full armor of God, so that when the day of evil comes, you may be able to stand your ground, and after you have done everything, to stand. Stand firm then, with the belt of truth buckled around your waist, with the breastplate of righteousness in place, and with your feet fitted with the readiness that comes from the gospel of peace."

Just then Jim hobbled up. "Hey, I like that. I think I'm going to buy myself one of those righteous Galahad breast protectors too. But where can I get a belt of truth? I hope it's not a chastity belt! Rose invited me to go with her to Barbados next month!"

41 THE REQUISITE HAPPY ENDING

As she promised, Diane Jones spearheaded the dismantling of Eden. The executive team worked with her as a cohesive unit to determine which pieces of the ECS software technology could be sold off to competitors. Those identified ECS software components were then "auctioned off" to the highest bidders. The shareholders were understandably not happy with the proceedings but, after a brief judicial hearing, it was determined that the shareholders would receive forty-nine cents on the dollar after the sell off of the ECS assets. The executive team consisting of Diane, Rose, and Ian, was then able to walk away with a sizable stipend from the sale of their shares. The big question for them was "what in the world do we do next?"

Ian McIntyre fulfilled his lifelong dream of visiting Tibet. Rather than exploring the Himalayas, he joined a small party on a tour of the Tibetan holy mountains, including Mount Kailash the "precious jewel of snows." Pilgrims believe that circumambulating Mt. Kailash is the right way to worship the god of the mountain and pray for good fortune and happiness.

After visiting "the god of the mountain" and concluding his Tibetan adventure, Ian returned to a bevy of job-offers. After careful consideration, he accepted a job offer at IBM's Watson Labs, in Yorktown Heights New York.

Detective Jim Kirkland went to Barbados with Rose Chen. They had a wonderful time together but concluded that they were really worlds apart in many respects and unsuited for a long-term relationship. They still remain friends and continue to see each other on a casual basis.

After her return from Barbados, Rose sought employment and was immediately offered a lucrative position as VP of sales for a Silicon Valley robotics venture. She is currently heavily involved in the introduction of workplace-oriented robots to the manufacturing industry.

Diane Jones elected not to pursue full-time employment; she is now spending more time with her family and consulting part-time. Her real interest, however, is the joint venture she created with Pastor Ted Johnson and Pastor Isaac White. Called techwarnings.org, their foundation is dedicated to warning consumers about their dependency on technology. The techwarnings website is now growing each day, with several active blogs and a daily example of technology gone awry.

Detective Jim Kirkland still partners with Detective Tony Magnini on the San Francisco police force. He remains active in Parkour training and hopes to be a certified trainer in the near future.

Detective Tony Magnini has become much more involved in activities at his church and is undergoing the education necessary to become a deacon.

Both Detectives Magnini and Kirkland were inspired by their experiences with Luci Ferguson and with ECS. With the help of budding novelists John Altson and Bob Lee, they are collaborating to write a book documenting all of their observations. They are hoping that it will be a best seller with movie rights, if they can resolve whether Luci was really Satan.

EPILOGUE

Lee Woo Yeun sat in his office at the Netslate headquarters in South Korea, staring at the envelope on his desk. Moments before he had been elated at learning of the demise of Luci Ferguson. He had been thinking that, at last, he was finally free of that devil woman, when in the morning mail he had discovered a package addressed from her.

I will NOT let her get her talons back into me, he snarled to himself. This is the final end here and now.

He opened the package, and a letter and a USB thumb drive spilled out onto his desk. He held up the letter gingerly with one hand, as if it was about to bite him, and turned around to his office shredder. He then unceremoniously dropped the letter into the slot in the top without reading it. For a few seconds, the shredder gave a long hideous howl as it chewed on Luci's words.

Woo Yuen then dropped the USB drive on the floor, and stomped on it with his heel over and over again until it was a jumbled mass of shards. He scooped the bits up and tossed them all in the trash.

The world is better off without any more of her hideous schemes, he thought, and he turned and looked at the rising sun shining down on his homeland.

The lieutenant hesitated before he knocked on the door. Which title was appropriate for him to use? Supreme Commander? Chairman? Marshal of the Democratic People's Republic of Korea? At least with His Excellency Kim Jong-il he could use that title or Eternal Commander. Perhaps Supreme Commander was best. He hesitantly knocked on the door.

"Enter," said Kim Jong-un, the leader of North Korea.

"Supreme Commander. I have here a most unexpected delivery from the United States. We have scanned it and it appears to contain some paperwork and a disc of some sort. It is addressed to you, Supreme Commander."

"Bring it here."

Kim Jong-un hated these interruptions. He had so many demands upon his time, and the military was still suspicious that he was unprepared to take over in his father's place. He needed to be very careful in how he handled matters with other countries.

He opened the package, and a letter slipped out.

"Dear soon-to-be Great Marshal of the Democratic People's Republic of Korea,

My name is Luci Ferguson. You may have heard of me. If not, a file on the enclosed disc labeled Luci-bio.doc will provide ample details.

In short, I am an expert in Artificial Intelligence (AI). The enclosed disc provides details on a product called Coach 6.0 It will provide you with technology with which you can harass and eliminate all of your enemies. It will also provide you with advanced AI technology that you can deploy to your military. Finally, the capabilities on this disc will allow your computer scientists to enable your strategic weapons to advance beyond even what is available in the United States.

I know that your country is beleaguered on all sides and that you have enemies within. With the information I have provided, you should finally be able to reach the title of Great Marshall, the same as your father, Kim Jong-il and grandfather, Kim Il-sung.

Time is short, and you must act quickly.

The world is yours for the taking.

Sincerely,

Luci Ferguson"

Kim Jong-un stared at the note. Even he had heard of this infamous Coach device. Because of sanctions on his country, he had not been able to obtain copies. Here was information that, perhaps, would enable him to fulfill all of his hopes and dreams.

"Lieutenant, I want you to immediately take this to our top computer scientists in the science wing. Tell them I order them to analyze the information, and wish to see a device within the week. I want you to personally oversee that they work twenty–four hours a day on this."

"Yes, Supreme Commander. I will make it so."

As the lieutenant closed his door, Mr. Kim got up and did a little dance. Yes, a little "What you please" dance is quite apropos, he mused as he imitated PSY's binocular moves. Soon I will see my enemies and they will be mine.

AFTERWORD: A PERFECT STORM

Luci, Lucifer, Satan, The Evil One, or whatever we call it, is merely a catalyst in this novel. Everything that happens to our characters, all the many lost souls, is very much capable of happening without any intervention. It may just be a matter of time.

Consider that we are ripe for what might be called "A Perfect Storm." There are four synergistic forces acting upon our global society that are poised to come together and bring about our ultimate undoing. These forces, in no particular order, are:

(1) Our unquestioning trust of the Internet, and the devices that feed off of it.

(2) The extent to which we are a pleasure-seeking society. If it feels good, we are apt to do it.

(3) Our children becoming desensitized to violence because of the pervasiveness of violence in all forms of media.

(4) The "Wild West" of personal privacy violations.

What's to be done? We need to be personally aware of these forces. We need to listen to our Superego, not just to our Id. We need to walk away from sex and violence in the media. We need to be prayerful. We need to, most of all, be a more loving culture.

CHAPTER NOTES, BY BOB LEE

Chapter 2

IBM's Watson program is the computer system that beat the top two past champions at the TV game show Jeopardy! The televised event was held over two days in February, 2011. IBM is working to develop a medical decision support system to aid doctors based on Watson. As far as we know, there are no plans to use Watson in the way we describe in this novel. Let us hope it doesn't come to what Ken Jennings wrote as his final answer, "I for one welcome our new computer overlords."

Chapter 3

One of Coach's functions is described as being able to analyze the "strength and mood" of statements in order to understand the emotion attached to a user's written comments. IBM Research has developed such a program.

Chapter 5

Many new technology products go through a painful startup. We tried to depict the inevitable meetings that happen where Marketing blames Development for not making a robust enough product, and Development blaming Marketing and Sales for not being able to sell it. And all complain that the product costs too much and the price should be dropped.

Chapter 6

An "angel investor" is similar to a venture capitalist, but invests his or her own funds. If you have seen the TV show "Shark Tank," those are angel investors. We especially liked applying this term to our devilish lady, Luci.

Chapter 7

I. I wrote computer gaming programs as part of my computer courses at Princeton University in the early 1970s. The procedures described are typical of how these gaming programs work. My college roommate and I also wrote a 3-D tic-tac-toe playing program that learned as you played it and ran into the "local maximum" problem described in the text. In the 1990s, I asked one of the IBM Research folks about this problem, and found out it still was unsolved.

These gaming programs use many expert 'rules of thumb'. One of the fun activities that I participated in was getting a copy of a simplified version of IBM's Deep Blue chess playing program that beat the world chess champ, Gary Kasparov. I even got to attend Game 5 of that historic match and still remember some of the shocked looks on the commentators and Kasparov as Deep Blue seemingly rejected all of these basic rules of thumb and somehow saved a losing position. Later, I would take the simplified version to high school chess clubs and let them modify the importance of the various rules of thumb, such as the value of a rook on an open file, and then let the club's version play the IBM version.

II. Luci mentions a number of programs in beta to help people improve their lives through gaming: Elm City Stories for the iPad which allows adolescents to react to sexual situations and see their risk of HIV; Massive Health's 'Eatery' which analyzes photos of people's meals; 'SuperBetter'; 'QuitNow!'and 'EveryMove.' These are all real programs.

III. Eliza, a psychoanalytical program, was a real program written by an MIT professor and is still floating around as one of a number of silly online chat bots. It is fairly famous in the AI annals.

IV. The MIT Professor anecdote about grad students feeling sorry for a computer if it apologized 'sincerely' is a true experiment. The story was related by the professor at an

IBM Research hosted conference on Human-Computer interaction.

V. The sad story (mentioned here and in Chapter 11) about the Korean couple who let their infant child starve while they fed their fake online child is a true story. You can find it by searching on Google. We in no way want to make light of this event, but we thought that it showed how powerful computer program addiction could be. A device like Coach would be even more seductive. Having Luci be involved as the impetus behind the child seemed appropriate.

Chapters 8 & 9

The legality of Coach should make you pause. There is no actual rule about gathering personal data and selling it. The USA has followed a self-policing policy for the companies doing this. What we included in the novel was best practices for a company to protect itself, such as separating out any personally identifiable information from the gathered data, and encrypting the personal information. When I created personalized systems 10 years ago at IBM, this was how it was implemented. Unfortunately, not all companies follow this approach. Witness the Sony PlayStation Network 2011 security breach where approximately 77 million members had their personal information hacked.

What is also worrisome in the news is that the companies selling the gathered information to others only will say that it is 'difficult' to track back the responses to a specific individual.

Chapter 10

You can buy the 4½ inch high Christian Louboutin 'Divinoche' red soled shoes for around $1,000. With a name like that, how could we NOT include them in the story as Luci's shoes?

Chapter 12

I. If you have ever had a technical problem with your computer, you might have experienced tech support 'taking over' your PC from a remote location to solve your problem. As far as we know, no one has done this with a smartphone, but there is no reason why they couldn't. Having Luci take over Billy's phone to talk to him as if she were his Coach system is a projection of using the same type of capability.

II. There are set punishments described in the literature for each deadly sin, and a specific demon is associated with each punishment. Beelzebub is the demon who delivers the punishment for gluttony, which is to be force-fed lizards, toads and snakes. It is why Billy chokes on frog's legs, and why Luci says the phase, "I'll be-Elsie-Bub eleh."

Chapter 13

I. The phrase, "Kill'em all, and let God sort'em out" is a paraphrase used by some elite military units. It is derived from a quote by Arnaud-Armaury, the Abbot of Citeaux, the Papal Legate, in approximately the year 1210. It occurred at a battle at Beziers, France, where Christian forces slaughtered tens of thousands of men, women and children accused of heresy. Abbot Arnaud was asked how to tell the heretics from the good Christians in the city. As recorded by a monk at the battle, he answered, "Kill them all. God will know His own."

II. Mammon is the demon in charge of meting out the penalty for greed, which is boiling in oil. Although most fire pits are run by gas, we used some creative license here with Sam's fire pit being run by oil. We wanted to make sure the punishment matched the sin.

Chapter 14

There are many apps currently available that are similar to the ones described on Billy's smartphone in the text. The names 'Pie Creator', 'Restaurant Story' and 'Bakery Time' are made up but very close to apps you can currently purchase.

Chapter 16

I. At one time, K-tel actually did sell Barbados "yellow bus" music. I am a proud owner.

II. The December 2012 issue of Scientific American Magazine has a short article describing how, in 2012, over ½ of the population in the USA now has a smartphone, and that most people don't know that almost all smartphones transmit their GPS locations by default. It also includes the term 'reality mining' for the process of culling information from that smartphone data. Mentioned are three true items extracted from the data about the most advertising clicks. They come from: 1) people sitting in movie theaters waiting for the movie to start. 2) fishermen waiting for a bite, and 3) people in general on a Sunday morning (shame on all of us).

When our novel was nearing completion, the FTC made the following statement about how smartphone apps are spying on our kids. They analyzed the top 400 apps in the Google and Apple stores and found that "nearly 60 percent of the apps transmitted the device's ID to the app developer, advertiser or other third party." The officials also found that 14 apps in addition transmitted the user's geolocation or phone number. Here is one of many articles on this story: http://thehill.com/blogs/hillicon-valley/technology/271965-ftc-warns-cellphone-apps-are-snooping-on-kids

Chapter 17

Tony's middle name, Benedetto, means "blessed."

Chapter 19

The method for preloading one person's personalized information so that multiple others can use it can be done under certain circumstances. We could do this with the IBM speech recognition software many years ago. The story about preloading a machine manufacturer's profile so that it would recognize unique maintenance manual wording upon first use is true.

Chapter 21

The CNN story is true that Congressman Kucinich lobbied at a special session of Congress to eliminate tax deductions to companies that contribute to childhood obesity:http://www.politifact.com/ohio/statements/2012/nov/26/dennis-kucinich/dennis-kucinich-says-tax-code-effectively-subsidiz/. It is also true that the sizes of Santa suits have increased by over 50%, and that the US Military has said that Americans are too fat to fight. It is the number one reason for not accepting someone into the military. The increase in snack food sales is fictional, and is meant to imply that the Coach system is contributing to gluttony based on Billy's profile data.

Chapter 22

I. The Washington Post story that Las Vegas celebrated its 79th anniversary of 'Repeal Day' is true including the former mayor's quote about it: http://www.lasvegassun.com/news/2012/dec/05/las-vegas-celebrates-79th-anniversary-repeal-day/. The quote attributed to the current mayor about the 'what happens in Vegas' ad campaign, as well as the increase in visitors in Vegas and Atlantic City, is fictional, and meant to imply that Coach is causing this based on Liz's profile data.

II. The traditional punishment for Eric's sin of Lust is to be smothered in fire and brimstone; of course, the Demon associated with this is Asmodeus.

Chapter 24

The CBS NEWS story about 'Tracking Sex Offenders' is true: See-> http://www.cbs47.tv/content/special_features/special_seri es/story/Special-Report-Tracking-Sex-Offenders/9kqOsobLIEyHz2x5Xdn57Q.cspx. It is a rising problem in California attributed in the article to the October 2011 mandate to reduce the prison population, and as a result, that the police are not arresting offenders who cut off their GPS ankle monitors. The quote from the San Bernadino Sheriff is fictional, and meant to imply that the offenders are learning they can get away with this from Coach.

Chapter 26

It is true that PSY's 'Gangnam Style' music video surpassed the online views of Justin Bieber's 'Baby' music video and received over one billion views on YouTube in only five months by the end of 2012 and is the most viewed video of all time. There have also been multiple parodies of it. You cannot fully appreciate this chapter if you haven't seen it, so go to YouTube and search on 'PSY Gangnam Style.'

Chapter 27

The genesis of this chapter 'The Gypsy' was that our family always has a Christmas grab bag, and one of the presents this year was a Magic 8 Ball, which I hadn't seen in years. I thought, *too bad it doesn't look like the devil*, and then it hit me what I had to write. Did this chapter seem a bit familiar? It is because it is an homage to an old 1960 episode of "The Twilight Zone" called "Nick of Time." In the episode, William Shatner plays a superstitious newlywed who enters a diner with his new wife when their car breaks down. At the table is a napkin holder with a demon head on top called 'The Mystic Seer' which, if you put a penny in and ask a yes/no question, and then push a lever, a piece of paper is ejected with the Seer's answer. As Shatner asks it questions, they all seem to come true and become more and more sinister. You should be able to find the episode on Netflix or Amazon video streaming as the 7th episode of season 2 of the series. Watch it. It is totally creepy and has a great ending.

Chapter 28

Mind mapping software actually exists, and is meant to stimulate problem solving as explained in the chapter.

Chapter 29

O le ali'i aso!" means "The Chief's Day" in Samoan. At least, that is the best we could do using online free translation software. We apologize to any Samoan's out there for mangling what seems to be a beautiful melodic language. The story about "The Chiefs Day" and the Cannibal Chief Malietoa is true and is an excerpt from the Robert Luis Stevenson museum's web site.

Chapter 30

AT&T, IBM, and Kurzweil all have text to speech software. Most of us have heard those robotic sounding voices. What you probably haven't heard is some of the astounding research on realistic computer voices. To hear some truly amazing computerized speech in multiple languages, visit the IBM Research website at: http://www.research.ibm.com/tts/

Chapter 32

I. Electroconvulsive Therapy, or ECT, also known in the past as 'Shock Treatment" is now a standard procedure for some symptoms such as depression. Research showed that anesthesia was key to making it a safe and reliable procedure, and as stated in the chapter recent papers have detailed how it works on the brain.

II. Patty's sin is 'Pride', since she is too proud to get help and thinks she can do it all herself. The punishment for pride is being 'Broken on the Wheel.' Thus, Patty is on a wheeled gurney, and the dials on the machine are 'wheel-like.'

Chapter 34

Ajmal's sin is 'Wrath' and the punishment for that is to be 'Dismembered Alive.' I personally feel bad for Ajmal. He didn't want to hurt anyone, and who wouldn't want to blow up his old boss' desk? But seriously – push the red button? Oh, Ajmal.

Chapter 35

The Swami tries to teach Chandra some of the 'Seven Virtues' to overcome her sin of 'Sloth.' Patience, Diligence (aka perseverance) and Temperance (aka self-control) are three of the seven virtues. The other four are: Chastity, Charity, Kindness and Humility. The penalty for Sloth is being thrown into a snake pit.

Chapter 37

I. The top online passwords that people use really are 'password', '123456' and 'abc123', and the 21st most used one is 'jesus' – please do not use simple easily guessed passwords!

II. Johnny's sin is 'Envy' and the punishment for that is being 'Immersed in Freezing Water.' The demon that administers the punishment is 'Leviathan' which is why Coach sinks into the leviathan deep.

Chapter 39

I. The chapter title is from a quote by Miguel De Cervantes: "Forewarned, forearmed; To be prepared is half the victory"

II. The Atheme ceremonial dagger is used in some black magic rites.

III. The Winchester 'Black Talon' bullets were initially sold to civilians, but due to an infamous San Francisco shooting in 1993, they henceforth were only sold to law enforcement and used until about 2001. Their black color was from a "Lubalox" paint-like lubricant. They were eventually replaced by the Ranger SXT line, whose bullets were not painted black, and more recently by the Ranger T-series.

Chapter 40

Some literature indicates that iron is painful to demons.

Chapter 41

There is no such site as techwarnings.org. Perhaps there should be.

EPILOGUE

As we finished the novel, IBM announced their '5 in 5' projections (search Google for 'IBM 5 in 5' or http://www.ibm.com/smarterplanet/us/en/ibm_predictions_for_future/ideas/index.html) which stated that in five years, smartphones would have all of our five senses included. You'll be able to smell any object you point at and your smartphone will simulate the sensation of touching something. Though there are many good things we could do with that, I still wonder what Eric (whose sin was 'Lust' and who was stalking the teenager Emily) would have done with those capabilities!

TOPICS FOR DISCUSSION

1. Before reading the Chapter Notes, did you think that Sam Washburn's vision for a "very smartphone" was attainable today? How about after reading the Chapter Notes?

2. Do you think privacy issues are presently being ignored? If yes, what dangers do you foresee?

3. Sam Washburn starts off as the major character and is killed by Luci later on. Was this a disappointment? Why?

4. What did you think of Luci's "communication through quadrants?" Some executives use this technique for interviews, you know.

5. Some of the "sinful characters" portrayed in the book are exaggerated profiles of people whom the authors knew. Did you think of people you knew?

6. Do you think that we rely on technology too much? If yes, do you see that getting worse over time?

7. Are you fearful about GPS tracking and its negative implications for criminals?

8. Do you believe that the forces of evil are real? Why?

9. Why do you suppose we still have keyboards on smartphones? Why can't we have a purely speech-driven interface?

10. Did you like the idea of "mind mapping" to solve problems?'

11. Do you believe in a spiritual realm as another dimension?

12. Do you believe that some people are "born bad," and

the evil can be a genetic disorder?

13. In the Epilogue, what do you think were the new features were that Luci added to Coach 6.0 when she sent it to North Korea? What would you have included?

ACKNOWLEDGEMENTS

Many thanks to:

George Altson for his religious insight

Barbara Altson, for her patience with her husband

Jane Lee, for her patience with her husband

Lori Lee, for being a supportive sister

Linda Bunker for her moral support

Ricky Sides for his publishing insights. Ricky is the author of a number of fiction books including the "Peacekeeper" series as well as books on women's self-defense and a husband's perspective on coping with breast cancer.

ABOUT THE AUTHORS

John Altson retired from IBM in 2010 after more than twenty years of exposure to IBM's cutting-edge technology. His involvement with IBM Research is reflected in many of the concepts put into play within his two latest novels, *The Id from Eden* and *Luke2*. Additionally, John has published two children's books: *What Happened to Grandpa? A child views the hereafter through the world's major religions* was published in 2009 and *The A to Z of Forgotten Animals* was published in 2010. John has a degree in mathematics from Hunter College in New York City and is a member of Pi Mu Epsilon, the Mathematics Honor Society. He has been called upon to be a guest lecturer at Harvard University.

Bob Lee retired from IBM after over 30 years with the company. During that time, he held various technical and marketing jobs, including product development, brand management and personalized web campaign development and deployment. His work with IBM Research included creating multiple versions of IBM's computer speech recognition products, as well as demonstrating a simplified version of IBM's Deep Blue AI computer program to high schools during National Engineering Week. Bob holds a degree in Electrical Engineering and Computer Science from Princeton University, and a Master of Science in Teaching (Mathematics) from Pace University. Bob also holds a 1st degree black belt in Taekwondo. This is his first novel, but he has been an avid reader of fantasy and science fiction literature since he was a child.

Made in the USA
Charleston, SC
29 January 2013